TRAIT

ABRACSIS

Front Cover design
Isaiah Xavier Bradley

TABLE OF CONTENTS

I dedicate this story to the wonderful people of many colors and traditions I've encountered at home and abroad. They're the angels who don't make the news, but are constantly an ever shining light in the life of a stranger during their time of need. People who prove over and over that there's more good than evil in this world, despite the evil seeming to always take center stage! They're responsible for this story of love, compassion and adventure. I thank every one of you for your faith in my ability and encouragement when I doubted myself! You know who you are!

Thank-you! Mahalo! Danke! Gracias! Arigatou! Asante! Merci! Ngiyabonga!

'We know not from whence we've come.
No worries where we're heading!'

THE PROPHECY

The Hopi believe in the hope of the Coming of the 5th Perfected and Final Age…Fulfillment. They believe it will bring about the restoration and eternal preservation of the Earth and correction of all life.

'It is written that when the Blue Star Kachina makes its appearance and we see halos around the heavenly bodies, the time has come when we must reform and those of us, like-hearted, must unite and rise up for survival.'

FOREWORD

JUNE 23RD

Seconds before midnight in Ryaahdi, Egypt, fifteen miles east, outside the city proper, is the El Ahabib Observatory. A new planetarium housing the latest advancement in telescopes, the Zeiss-902 and the AZT-15. Seated inside, in captain-style recliners surrounded by monolithic screens that lend the illusion they're floating amidst the stars while being serenaded by mechanical melodies, are Drs. Isaiah Buhari and Amalee Dashar. Both share a deep passion to discover worlds beyond and their combined genius enhances the probability of their success. They've been a team for five years.

Amalee rears back, stretches and checks the time…11:59 p.m. He lowers his head in mock submission and sighs, "Another monotonous shift, Eye!" *That's the nickname he'd given Buhari.* Eye exhales and looks to him, "Well, Lee! Look on the bright side! There's tomorrow and the guys (Drs. Martin Sakara and Fareed Basheer, their reliefs) will be here soon!" Eye's first to notice an unfamiliar sound and begins looking about! "Lee, do you hear that?" "Hear what?" "Sssh…listen!" It grows louder and Lee hears it. They begin to visually and physically search for its source. It's when they move toward the printers that they see pages rapidly expelling! Small mounds have already formed and are growing taller! They're transfixed by shock! The signal carrying the data isn't coming from any location on *Earth*! It's coming from somewhere out there! They look to each other excitedly! "I can't believe this is happening!" shouts Amalee giddily! Eye smiles as he shifts his eyes to the star-filled screens, "Oh! Believe it! They've sent a message!"

CHAPTER ONE
consequence

Earth's not the result of a cosmic collision, but she is one of a kind!

Two million years ago the citizenry of the planets within the Mahos galaxy were participating in the historic Jubilee of the Galactic Institute of Knowledge, affectionately referred to as the 'G.I.K'. It's a unique knowledge storehouse filled with detailed information of other species and civilizations. To envision its magnitude consider the merging of the Daido Institute of Technology, Fudan University, Massachusetts Institute of Technology, Taiwan Science Institute, Tesla Research Center, USC-Berkley, University of Pennsylvania and the University of Science and Technology of China into a single entity!

There's been inter-planetary pageantry, feasting, dancing and planet hopping for the past 840 metos or 25 earth days. It's a 'luau' type celebration on steroids! The official period of the 'jubilee' celebration is 872 metos or 26 earth days. The apex of the celebration has arrived! The ceremony of commencement!

During its proceeding nine post graduate Almadians, of the Quopozoest clan, are dispensed multiple doctorates in the fields of quantum genetics, zelphon physics, Xtol engineering, nano-spectronics, quasi-nuclear biology, Kevon chemistry and Sesal molecular science. This is unprecedented and the *G.I.K* has no rewards commensurate to their accomplishments! However, the *'Many'* have been in observance and highly impressed by the works of the nine! *They* conference and agree to offer them the privilege of collaboration on the construction of a *'life sphere'*... *a* new world! An honor never before proffered! *They* send forth the 'feminine genderplex' from amongst them to extend the privilege.

The student body and faculty are proud and praise the success of their classmates, friends and students! Except the Bahleide. They're a grotesque, foul smelling, blood-sucking, cannibal race that lacks high level intelligence and pigmentation. The latter circumstance renders them 'light,' just shades away from transparency! They're in attendance under strident conditions and required to wear customized uniforms to obscure their countenance and odor! None of their bonah has ever graduated due to their severely deficient IQs and they burn with envy!

The ceremony's ended. Persons of varying *species* are mingling about congratulating the graduates, honorees and socially interacting when a strange, sweet fragrance fills the air! A greenish cloud suddenly appears! A wide greenish beam emits from it and splashes onto the surface creating a beach ball size circle that expands outwardly to the diameter of a circus ring! There's a burst of blinding light! When it wanes a gigantic, beautiful 'Lotus' sits inside the circle! Its petals are snow white and leaves vibrant green! All in proximity stand transfixed, at ease, in wonderment! Except the honorees! Their oculi sparkle! They're smiling and nodding as if seeing and hearing something the others cannot! And they are! After all, h*er* presence *is* for them! Only they can see *her* oculi and many versions of smiles! The outer edges of *her* pedals glow as *she* communes in a soft, melodic, soothing tone (*they're able to hear and translate*) congratulating, praising and extending the privilege. Each greets *her* humbly with salute! They accept and implore *her* to express their respect and gratitude to the *others* and salute once more. A blinding flash occurs and *she's* gone! *Rarely did 'The Many' physically manifest! Indeed this was a momentous event! (The Many = Divine Omnipotent Ones aka the D.O.O. = THE CREATORS)*

Despite Bahleide attempts of sabotage the *life sphere's* launched to a location within the void specified by the *D.O.O.*

While *it's* undergoing evolutionary metamorphosis the honorees assist with the construction of new lifeforms, accessories of a kind, to love, respect, maintain and with *discipline* populate *it*. After providing the 'life element' for the new forms, in honor of the Almadians the *D.O.O.* infuses them with modified traits of their bonah…human.

Sixteen hundred ecru, black, brown, green, red, tan, yellow and violet, male and feminine, embryos are created in the hues of *Earth*. *There're no 'light'*. Despite constant guard an un-authorized entry's discovered in the laboratory. An immediate lock down ensues and the process of determining specimen integrity begins. Unfortunately, there's been contamination! It appears minimal. Three hundred and two are compromised and fully infected with the Bahleide trait. *At maturation they'll lack pigmentation.* They'll be imposters bearing the likeness of Almadian beings, but possess Bahleide ideology, behavior and mental processes. *Real body snatchers!* The infected embryos have discolored, darkened and are easily extracted from the pearly sea! However, fifty-two sets (m/f) of the three hundred and two have been minimally effected. They've retained their Almadian composition but at maturity they'll lack pigmentation.

This is an appalling act of treachery by the Bahleide! Their audacity to interfere will someday bring a wrath of epic proportions upon their world!

Seventy-five helooses later (*750 earth* years), the Almadian armada travels to the designated place in the void where the *sphere* had come to rest with more than fifteen hundred scientists, two thousand support/technical personnel, one thousand utility aircraft and other transport. As they clear the dark side of the moon before them is a huge orb spotted with large and small patches of blue, blotches of brown and green surrounded by white, wispy clouds. It rotates slowly as if suspended by an invisible string against a dark, star filled curtain! They're ecstatic by what they see and name *her*, *Earth*. *Her* landmass is whole! There's no fragmentation, no continents, only a solid mass with an abundance of lakes, ponds, rivers, streams and mountains. The entirety of *her* landmass is easily explored from east to west, north to south by foot at this time! *Her heart rests in what's now Midwestern North Americas and her respiratory systems in South Americas!*

As the armada enters *her* exosphere *she's* awakened! Not by the presence of the ships, but the spirits contained within them! As a newborn smiles into the faces of its parents, *she* begins to bloom! What'd been small patches of dark brown begin to color over with lush, green grasses and foliage across *her* surface. Flowers of every variety begin to bud and bloom, as well as, the fruit of the soil, vines and branches of trees! *Her* explosion's an amazing sight displayed on monitors thru out the fleet! No doubt *she* recognizes *one of her* creators (parents) and *delights* in their arrival!

Construction begins immediately on temporary research/neo-natal facilities for cultivation, development and harvesting (*birthing*) of the neonates in Kenya, Africa and other locations. When *they're* completed incubators are transferred from the ships. While awaiting half of the embryos to harvest and attain maturity the others are placed in suspension. During this time erection begins on the 'permanent outpost'. At this place a minimum of two Almadian officers will serve, alternating voluntary tours (one hundred earth years) as *Earth Monitors* for all *her* life. Observing, recording, inspecting, examining *her* condition and forwarding reports to command...Phakilra. The outpost will be camouflaged by fruit orchards, farm lands, vineyards, ranch for breeding equine and raising prime livestock for 'live' sale. *They did not and would not slaughter!* They chose honorable occupations capable of generating great profits that would afford them justifiable isolation from the *outside* world in the future.

Twenty weeks later...

The first generation of 'Tauri' (males) tear thru the fibrous walls of their bubble-like cocoons, full termed and execute their first involuntary action... breathing on their own! The Almadians are enamored with the clingy, wriggling little creatures of varying features and hues who're much smaller than their neonates! Some have elongated skulls like them! *The males are harvested first. Their role is to prepare for the arrival of the feminine. To protect and support them and in the future assist in the reproduction process.* They're nurtured with exceptional adoration, gentleness and patience! The Almadians are intrigued by the level of their intelligence! They're highly cognizant and learn as quickly by oration as they do thru observation! They begin to speak at seven months, walk and run at eight months and are hygiene independent at nine months, begin dressing themselves at eleven months and at fifteen months speak and understand an average of eight languages fluently! They're the epitome of 'show and tell'! The Almadians reveal *Earth's* mysteries to them to ensure *her* survival and endow them with other talents to ensure evolutionary progress and survival! They remain with them for two heloose.

The *feminine genderplex* infused more than half of the embryos with its essence! Therefore, they're feminine by nature and superior!

During maturation and education they present them with a very special gift from the *D.O.O....the 'Compendium'*. It's an infinite compilation of knowledge in the form of tantalum-like orbs pertaining to everything of *Earth* for the advancement of future generations with strong emphasis on reproduction discipline. *Population control.* Teaching them to live in balance with *her* and increase their knowledge to enable them to construct vessels and navigate their way back to Phakilra. The orbs of the 'Compendium' are activated by Tauri touch, only they can absorb their knowledge! *Encyclopedias are examples of the BT's vain attempts to emulate it!*

Confident they're leaving the Tauri in good order they collect all equipment before boarding, leaving only the first monitors behind. The moment the last ship departs *Earth's* solar system marks the beginning of Tauri independence. When the Armada returns to Phakilra each ship presents an impressive audio visual presentation of *Earth* and their experiences to the populous of the planets in the Mahos galaxy! Feasts are held in celebration of the birth of their *new child*, *Earth*. During and after the celebration more than eight-hundred cadets and twice as many senior officers volunteer for future duty as *Earth* monitors!

The Bahleide were given the most inhospitable, undesirable areas on *Earth* (Europe and the northern most regions of China and Japan) specified by the *D.O.O.* to *seed* the embryos they'd contaminated. They must vacate *her* and *her* solar system after one heloose! The Almadians and the *D.O.O.'s* expectations were extremely hopeful they'd perish due to lack of intelligence or harshness of environment!

The Tauri lived by the '*Compendium*' and their population was balanced, defect-free, intelligent and strong! Education was not only free, but a way of life. Their belief was that an advanced civilization could only be proficient if all within it were highly knowledgeable. Teachers were held in the highest esteem! After all, it was their responsibility to prepare the future! For more than ten thousand years the Tauri lived in peace and prosperity under matriarchal rule before the 'Great Upheaval' in 2968 B.C. It was at this time that BTs under the tutelage and command of a group of Bahleide, who'd defiantly remained on *Earth* and planned the assault against the Tauri! It was a horrific slaughter! They'd never encountered any BTs and assumed they hadn't survived! Much less had an army! They were unprepared when they set upon them! The green and violet Tauri were expunged! During the battle twelve descendants of the first lineage… *seedlings* were mortally wounded! They'd been *her* first born! However, the Bahleide were only successful in the destruction of their flesh. The *D.O.O.* had captured each of their souls and hid them in the safety of the '*sotia*, collected specimens of their genetic elements and re-inserted them at the end of the life chain for rebirth!

Thousands of Almadian officers have served successful, uneventful tours since the first so long ago. At the onset of the seventeenth century the first of the twelve is *reborn*. Immediately a supreme declaration's issued demanding search and retrieval of the others to follow! It becomes synonymous with the primary duty. The motivational element attached to the location of just *one* is immediate termination of duty, promotion and return to Phakilra!

Maj. Benjamil Quopozoest and Maj. Cathy Orkurokais are selected for duty during the latter part of the seventeenth century. Their home world is triple the size of *Earth*! They'd grown up and resided thousands of miles away from each other and they'd not attended academy together. They were total strangers upon their first meeting! Over time they became an excellent team and not only made friends, but became lovers. They joined and became Maj. Ben and Maj. Cathy Quopozoest. *Ben changed their surname to Beal for reasons of security.*

Nathaniel and Dora Beal are propelled into the realm of existence (*reborn*) thru Ben and Cathy at the outpost on July, 7, 1800 and July 7, 1802 respectively. Early in the life of the young ones two concessions are made regarding their safety. The first at the time of Dora's re-entry. The second was the painful decision to return to Phakilra without the children because the Bahleide were getting closer to uncovering their identities. They feared they'd discover their location and existence of the young ones. Reluctantly, they left them in the care of Tamesh and Mobahi, 'keepers'. The ideal guardians to care for, educate, train and guide them to the age of knowledge.

Nate and Doe as they affectionately refer to one another are reared out of foreign and public eyes. Their immediate circle of friends and confidantes are the descendants of ancestral Tauri generations. Their developmental environment's the village, the private corporate university and the expansive property, one hundred and fifty thousand acres, of the 'Greenwood Corporation'. These conditions are as essential for their protection as the concessions that'd been made in the past for them! Bahleide were still on the 'blood hunt'! Presently, four remain lost and roam the *Earth* unaware of their heritage!

They're the current monitors and on the short end (*twenty years*) of their second tours and greatly desire to locate a *seedling* on their watch!

To the world they're reclusive, philanthropic, single, sibling billion-aires. Nate's quite handsome! But few have ever glimpsed Dora's face! Their wealth's a combination of the legendary Rosewood vineyards, world famous thoroughbred breeding ranch, Stone Valley and their uncle's import/export enterprise and North Americas estate, 'Angel Place'.

CHAPTER TWO
the earth monitors

APRIL 22ND
Hurricane Mills, Tennessee

Situated on twenty thousand acres of rolling hills abundant of whitetail deer and turkeys, sprinkled with fresh water streams filled with sturgeon, mussels and trout, thirty miles south of Chattanooga is 'Angel Place'. The sprawling, eco-friendly, complex rests deep (five miles) inside the property from its entrance off of Route 64. 'Riders of Ancient Wings' (one of her favorite jazz selections) flows thru the audio on the first floor, official business area. Her heavy, high-heeled, footsteps are muffled by the Persian runner of the marble floor as she walks down the corridor to his office cradling folders in her arm. He wears a facial expression of confusion eyeing the screen before him as she enters. She seats herself before him and casts a concerning glance, "Something wrong?" *He casts her a piercing stare!* "Yes! I've no new acquisitions, investments nor ventures to validate this! What'd you do? Doe? What've you done? Rosewood's on track to gross a billion in sales! What're we selling? Where's this money coming from?" "Oh, Nate! Come on! You know I don't do illegal anything! How could you entertain the thought? You **really** don't know?" she retorts eyes flashing! *Now he's really baffled!* "It's wine sales! Nate, we've a new product! It's been on the market for two years!" She goes on to explain. "Several years ago while Tamesh and I were preparing mother's files for storage relocation. I noticed a box labeled, 'MOI'. Curious, I set it aside. Weeks later I reviewed the notes that were inside. Then ran a few tests and simulations for analysis. There was no doubt! Mother had discovered something wonderful! She'd developed a hybrid grape, sweeter, yielding 115% more anti-oxidants and delivering 88% of it directly into the blood stream upon consumption! Its skin's thinner and easier to digest. I catalogued the final product as 'Cathy' in honor of her." *Regretful of his harsh tone and insinuating questions he lowers his eyes and softens his voice.* "Please forgive me! That's wonderful Doe! But why didn't you tell me about this before now?" "Because it was during the erection and testing of the network globes. You and Jonas were focused on the task as expected!" *He recalls the hustle and bustle of that time and nods. Her degree of consideration causes him to smile!* "Oh, yes! I remember now! You're really something! A woman's woman and a man's man! I'm glad you're here!" "Yes. Me too! Nate! Getting back to the wine I sent you! You never opened it?" "Opened it?" "Yes! Opened it!" "No! But I will! Where is it?" "It's sitting right over there on the corner of the bar where it's been sitting for quite a while!" He casts a glance, "Doe! There's nothing there but a beautifully carved box of shot glasses." *She exhales sharply.* "Nate! That's not shot glasses! It's the wine!" He rises, retrieves the box, returns to his desk and opens it. Nestled in foam molding covered by white satin's a crystal goblet with his initials, corkscrew and a black matte bottle with a pink foil label bordered with detailed silver angelic wings affixed to it. In its center the word '*Cathy*' in italicized lettering. He uncorks it and slowly inhales its bouquet, "This is heavenly!" he praises before pouring some into the goblet. He swirls it about gently and sips, "Hmmm, my word! You've really outdone yourself! It's healthy, elegant and fun! But most importantly, it's Mum!" "It's admirable of you to toot my horn! But your breeding and management of the equines has been exemplary, to say the least! You've produced hundreds of champions!" "Yes, I surprise myself! Although I must admit it's been more than satisfying to see my theories and plans come to fruition! Uh...what is it?" "What's what?" "The reason why you're here?" "Oh!" *She offers the folders. He accepts glancing to her.* "Doe? You seem a bit gloomy. Want to talk about it? Tell me why?" *She exhales deeply.* "Nate! When Abamah, the first Tauri of coloration was elected COTA (Chief of the Americas) it rekindled the spirit of hope within me that possibly the Tauri's 'KSCs' were unlocking naturally from the blockage instilled thru generational programming by Bahleide and enforced by BTs. However, my hopes were very short lived! In less than a year there was the mass shooting at Bluewood Elementary school and still other tragedies, the island of Puerto Ricas hit with Lulu, a category seven tropical storm and the Sonoma fires roared in Californias! The arrogance of the Bahleide to disrespect and treat *her* with such cruelty really angers me! It's becoming more difficult and painful to watch them cultivate hatred and goad their minions to inflict mental and physical scars upon *her,* while our hands are bound, twenty-four hours a day, decade after decade, century after century! Nate! I can't wait to leave here! With each passing day I'm more unwilling to execute the duty I swore to honor! I want to leave now!" "Your feelings are justified! Doe! I share them too! I've been silent because I didn't want to worry you with my upset! If I could have my way they'd be exterminated for what they've done to *her!*" "What a lovely thought! I wish it were possible too! But they've a fate of their own!" "I know! I'm also baffled that Tauri males fail to realize that *Earth's* a reflection of *her* creator! *She* bears the *femme persona,* a christening of sorts by the *D.O.O.* validating the feminine as the superior! You know? I think we're both feeling the effect of 'LDTS' syndrome. I've only heard mention of it briefly. It's a depressive state brought on by the feeling of failure and longing to return home. That must be what we're experiencing. Think about it! We're almost to the end of our second tours and still we've been unsuccessful at locating even *one!* I guess the reality of going home empty-handed is causing the imbalance of our bio-rhythms and our anxiety levels to spike." *She hunches her shoulders and shakes her head.* "Nate, you're probably right! We're just frustrated! I really believed we'd find *one* though! Especially after enlisting Michael!" "Yes, Doe! He's an excellent tracker and has presented us with many candidates. It's not his fault they weren't *who* we sought! Anyway, the lure of early termination has long been in the rearview for us! We can self-terminate our duty though! There's no dishonor! Very few monitors have actually completed a second tour! Much less served as much time as we have! But our time remaining's a walk in the park at this point!"

"No! Nate, I know we must persevere, but it's bittersweet. Oh! Uh…speaking of Michael have you heard from him? I haven't in a while!" His brow wrinkles with suspicion. "Odd, you should ask! I spoke with him earlier. He wishes you well, as always! Listen? Am I going to have a problem as far as you're concerned?" "Whoa! Your protection mode's in overdrive! He's a gentleman, a great guy, excellent co-worker and v-e-r-y good friend!" "Yeah? Well, that may be how you see it! But I sense he feels differently! And…he is a handsome fellow!" "Oh! Nate stop! You're over reacting! Trust me! So what did he say?" "Well, uh…he's data on two candidates for our immediate review. But there're two more of interest to him!" "Hmp! I guess that's encouraging." she comments unmoved. "We can't give up! Not now!" he returns before goading, "Has Heather called lately?" *The question startles her!* "Why?" she challenges with a slight grimace. He stares to her, "Doe? Is there um…something I should-?" "She's not a problem really! She's just misguided! Nate! I'll take care of her! Hey? You're unusually edgy! What did you do? Look at their news broadcasts?" *He lowers his eyes in silence.* "Nate!" she scolds sympathetic. "Doe, I don't know what made me do it! (Previous monitors had created journals, documenting events and changes they'd witnessed. To inform and present those to follow a clear view of what had and was occurring to Earth and her children! They detested all humanoid broadcasts because they were always noir! Their chronicles confirm that after the Great Upheaval the Bahleide influence went unchallenged and infected the Tauri generations more and more with each passing century. Peace has unraveled at an unbelievable rate as Bahleide gnawed at its fabric like mice and devoured the psychology of hope as termites! The BTs were equally rabid!)* Uhh…when're you going back home?" "How'd you know I was planning to return?" "Oh! That was easy! You never stay here long! As a matter of fact, this is the longest you've stayed in a while!" *She looks to him with a smile!* "I'm leaving tomorrow. Why don't you come? It'd be a wonderful surprise! They'd love to see you and I promise we'll return within a week! Plus, we could check on the vineyards, the university and research facility!" *'He's never seen her so discontented! Is her offer an unspoken plea?'*

he ponders. "Okay!" *His answer startles her!* "You're really coming with me?" "Yes. What time are we leaving?" "As soon as I pay the ransom!" *He laughs!* "That's right! I'd forgotten about that! One can only wonder what they'll demand this time!" *They share laughter!*

Michael Fenfox

Ex-Marine, expert with weaponry and demolitions, martial arts master, multi-lingual, well-traveled and single. Six feet, six inches, two hundred and forty-five pounds, light-blue eyes, salt and pepper wavy hair (more pepper than salt) and a sun-kissed body built by nature with little help from the gym. Many years ago he'd answered a head-hunter's call for a 'security specialist' at Angel Place. He'd handled the matter so proficiently they offered him a permanent position in the corporation and solicited his help in their search for the *seedlings.* Since that time he's become an integral part of the corporation…he's family. His composite was confirmed shortly after his hiring. He's 96.7% Tauri.

1:30 p.m. Apr 22nd

Encompassing fifteen acres of manicured emerald green grass, a short distance from the main complex, are the state of the art, climate-controlled, oxygen-enhanced stables accented by cedar and wrought iron works. Juan's storing blankets when she enters. "Good-morning, Juan! How's everything? Okay?" He smiles, "Good-morning, Ma'am! Oh! Yes! Everything's fine! They've been fed, watered and groomed." She chuckles, "That's very well! But I'm not here to check on you! I'm here to visit with them!" *He blushes a bit and shakes his head!* "Of course! My luck ain't dat good!" he comments before exiting. She smiles briefly at his words, then enters each stall, withdraws three big red apples from the white sack she carries, places them on the hay covered floor and leaves their gates open. *She'd stopped by the kitchen en route.* "Good-morning!" she greets. They nod their heads a bit and begin to eat! After chomping on his apple, Prince, the copper colored Arabian, peeks his head out, shakes it gently from side to side and comments, "Hmp! Hmp! Hmp! That was s-o-o good! Thank-you! But Madam! Have you no decency? Have you no heart? He barely breathes in your presence! Have you never taken notice?" he taunts! "I must agree. That was straight out c-o-l-d-blooded!" comments her horse, Shaka, the jet black Friesian stallion. Zephyr, a saddle brown Peruvian Paso with a long golden mane (Nate's) snickers! "Come on! What's this about?" "Wait! You know we understand you, right? We can *feel* your loneliness! You need and want love! You're lonely! But to this very moment no one has come into our presence or yours worthy of you or able to fulfill your needs! Juan's nice and we kid you about him! But you do require something, someone more!" *She stares to them.* "Oh! Great wizards! Please tell me more!" "Doe! This is not a joke! We intend you no upset! But the one you need and seek is coming! Just be patient a little longer!" Shaka urges in a tone she's never heard! "Okay! Enough of the naysayer stuff! We're going to 'Greenwood'!" "Yeah, yah!" exclaims Shaka. "Oh yes!" says Prince. "Groovy!" comments Zephyr. Doe stands stunned by their reactions! As if hit by a brick Shaka pauses, "Uh…oh! I guess that means we're travelling on the '*Whisper*'?" "Uh…yea, yah!" "Hmm! Then there're conditions that must be met in order for us to travel!" *Her eyebrow rises.* "How'd I forget that! What're they again?" "Well, they've changed! First I require a twenty-two ounce glass of 'Johnny Walker Blue' on the rocks and four burgers with the works, hold the onions. Prince requires two pitchers of Canadian 'Cream Ale', four burgers with the works and fries and Zephyr requires three large pizzas, one cheese pepperoni and two mozzarella with spinach, mushrooms and a forty ounce diet Coke!" She looks to each of them skeptical! "You gotta be kidding! Are you guys serious?" "Oh yes! As a heart attack!" "This is blackmail!" "Call it what you want! They're our conditions!" She nods her head in resignation and sighs, "Alright. I'll get started on your orders!"

THE WHISPER

Not Xelinak Aircraft of the Czech Republic, Sabaretta Company of St. Louis, Missouri, North Americas, Bolling Aeronautics of Montessia, California, North Americas nor Macchi Aero of Forensio, Italy have plans either on drawing boards or laptops equivalent to the design of the 'Whisper'! It's an aero-space engineer's dream! A spectacular example of advanced engineering and design! It bears slight symmetry of a 'Manta' ray. Smooth, no tell-tale signs of abridgement and constructed of an element stronger than any known on *Earth*! It's one hundred and eighty-five feet in length, twenty-five feet width. The cabin's twenty feet wide and eight feet floor to ceiling. It weighs little more than two city buses and its energy source's a mind-bending marriage of solar, sodoenium and mercury = cold fusion! It's quiescent, hovers, cloaks and reaches speeds over five hundred miles per hour in less than twenty seconds! It's totally undetectable by any earthly means! A marvel and a real 'ghost'! It travels from Angel Place to the 'Greenwood, in the exosphere, in less than five hours!

7:10 p.m. They're loaded into the 'Whisper' without incident. She inspects their conditions before lift-off. They're secure and resting peacefully! *She'd added a gentle sedative to their apple treats! They didn't like traveling on the 'Whisper', but the other options, going thru the portal or the arduous journey via the sea, were definitely off the table!* The craft cloaks and lifts-off at 7:30.

Three and a half hours later…

Its 6:45 a.m. (EAT), the next day in Kenya when the craft lands on the 'Rosewood's' tarmac. Mother Nature welcomes them with *kusi,* monsoon rains! Prince, Shaka, and Zephyr are still asleep and easily extracted and transported to the stables. *This was a routine procedure for the grounds crew.* Doe and Nate dash thru the rain to a vehicle a few feet away. He climbs into the driver's seat and turns the key in the ignition while Doe scrambles into the passenger side.

They'd traveled this road many times and each time had always felt like the first! But this time's very different. It's absent the active sounds of nature and their way's not lit by the rising sun! At the crest of the hill he brakes and idles for a moment. They look down into the valley thru the watery windshield and smile to each other! Camouflaged by trees and shrubbery's the village…home! Soft glows emanate thru the greenery from a structure that sits farthermost north. It's the place of their childhood and the glows are streaming from the bamboo windows of their rooms! He continues and parks as close as possible to the steps of the verandah. They dart from the vehicle, up the steps onto the landing, remove their footwear and tip-toe thru the door. All's still inside. Sparingly placed fire lamps light their way! When they arrive to their rooms several large pillar candles burn brightly, fresh flowers have been placed about, their beds are turned down and an aromatic scent fills the air! A note rests on each pillow:

"Welcome home! Enjoy your bath. Be well!" signed 'Tah' and 'Bahi'. *Both smile at the signage. It's reflective of the time when they were very young and not yet able to fully pronounce their names.* They disrobe, bathe and crawl into bed. At home and at peace they nestle their heads into their pillows and are quickly lulled to sleep by the rhythm of *her tears*!

April 23rd

10:26 a.m. (EAT)

The sky's lightened a bit, but the rain continues! Leilani and Tahjere have set the table and a fresh arrangement of 'Birds of Paradise' sits at its midst. Finished cooking Tamesh and Mobahi move to the back porch to relax and enjoy their breakfast beverages (coconut milk, tea and coffee) while they await Doe and Nate. *Leilani and Tahjere are upperclassmen at the 'Greenwood' University who'd demonstrated the highest degree of excellence in culinary skills and etiquette proficiency during exams at the close of the semester. Their reward was five thousand dollars cash, six week residency in the guest quarters of the main edifice and the honor of providing food service (acquisition, inventory of provisions, planning/preparing meals and setting service/décor) for Tamesh and Mobahi. They'd earned one of the highest honors!*

Clad in robes and slippers they descend the stairs and enter the hallway a little after 11 a.m. There're no signs of Tamesh, Mobahi nor sounds of commotion! They continue thru the house to the dining area. It's prepared for service, but empty! They look to each other with a *knowing* and make their way to the back porch. Tamesh and Mobahi *feel* their presence and rise from their seats. They wear broad smiles as they move toward each other! Tamesh embraces Nate and Mobahi embraces Doe affectionately! After a long moment they switch. "It's wonderful to have both of you at home! You look well!" Tamesh exclaims! Mobahi gently pushes Nate away from him, "Turn around! Let me look at you! I've missed you, my son!" "No, Bahi! I've missed you more!" returns Nate chuckling! "Tah? Are you getting younger? What're you eating? What're you drinking?" Doe muses. Chuckling Tamesh shakes her head, gives an inspective look and takes her hand, "Come! We've prepared both of your favorites!" *Doe and Nate smile to each other!* As the group heads back inside Leilani and Tahjere approach, bow their heads and place their right hands over their hearts in military salute position, hand up and outward. Lifting their heads they address, "Your Highness! Can we be of service?" All the while their eyes are glued on Doe and Nate! They've knowledge of them, but it's the first time seeing them, up close and personal and they're enchanting creatures! Tamesh introduces them and informs, "They're the winners of this semester's competition! They'll be coming to 'Angel Place' in the future for internship with Maxx, Jamie and Petra." Doe and Nate bow their heads, salute and bid them eloquent congratulations! By their expressions the students are clearly overwhelmed by their display of homage to them! Looking to Nate, Tamesh offers, "Want to try them out? See what they can do?" "Yes! That's an excellent idea! I'm calling the men together this evening! They could prepare our feast!" Tamesh looks to them, "Are you ready for such a task?" Speechless, they smile and nod anxiously! "Okay! I'll summon you later for advisement! Right now we're hungry! Leilani, Tahjere? Would you like to join us?" They smile acceptance! Everyone enters the kitchen and fills their plates. Seated in the dining room they give thanks to *Earth* and the *D.O.O.* then begin eating!

Half an hour passes before Nate wipes his mouth and hands vigorously, folds the napkin and lays it across his empty plate. His hunger satisfied, he rises, moves to Tamesh, nestles his head in the crux of her neck, his face against hers and hugs her tenderly for a long moment. *His love for her is felt around the table!* "Tah! Man, oh man! The food was delicious as always! I've really missed it and I've missed you! Thank-you!" She places her hands lovingly on his arms about her neck, turns her head slightly and looks into his eyes dotingly, "You're more than welcome, dear one!" As he moves to Mobahi thunder claps and rains pummel the roof! Tamesh glances to the ceiling then back to both men. They *know* that *look*! Nate nods to him, "I guess that means we're grounded! No feast!" *Mobahi nods with a fake grimace.* "Come, my son!" The men leave the room embracing each other's shoulder speaking softly and chuckling! Tamesh looks to Leilani and Tahjere, "When you're finished your duties take your leave. No worries about the evening meal!" "Thank-you! Highness! We hope to one day cook like you! Thank-you!" they bid saluting. Doe smiles at their truthful flattery! *'Smart kids!' she ponders.* "They're fine specimens, Tah!" "Yes! They're good! Now, my dear is our time! Your room or mine?" *Doe smiles!* "Yours of course! It's got more charm, a better view and a wet bar!" *Tamesh chuckles!* "I was hoping you'd make that choice because I'd like you to mix me a 'Lotus'!" *They chuckle!*

Doe prepares their drinks, moves to the cozy couch, hands Tamesh her glass and seats herself child-like next to her. Tamesh takes a sip. "Hmm, child! You fix a mean drink! This is really good! *She places her arm about Doe's shoulder.* Now tell me true! What's your discomfort?" *Doe looks to her with sad eyes.* "Tah? Nate's spoken to you of me hasn't he?" "Yes. He worries for you!" *She grimaces a bit.* "Tah! They won't stop hurting *her* and we're forbidden to help *her*! It's amazing *she's* survived the injuries they've caused thus far! *(October 10, 1957 -Windscale fire-British nuclear accident worse than Three Mile Island; January 17, 1966-Palomares Incident; January 21, 1968; December 18, 1970-Yucca Flat; July 10, 1976- Seveso explosion releases a deadly Dioxin cloud; 1978- Love Canal toxic industrial waste disaster; March 28, 1979- Three Mile Island; December 2-3, 1984 pesticide plant explosion; April 26, 1986- Chernobyl nuclear explosion; August 10, 1985- K-431 Chazhma Bay Russian nuclear submarine explosion; September 13, 1987-Goiania Accident; March 24, 1989-Exxon Valdez oil spill; January and February 1991- Kuwait oil fires; April 6, 1993- Tomsk-7 explosion; September 30, 1999- Tokaimura nuclear plant- worse nuclear disaster before Three Mile Island; April 2010- The Aral Sea- water decimation; April 20, 2010- Deep Water Horizon- Gulf of Mexico oil spill; March 11, 2011- Fukushima Daichi nuclear disaster and the Minamata Disease- industrial poisoning.)* I fear *she* won't be able to counter their next attack!" *Tah lowers her eyes for a moment before returning them to her.* "I understand your feelings! But you must remember *she's* enduring! You and the Tauri feminine of the world must also be as enduring! Remember all positive energy invigorates *her*! Now! Would you pour me another Lotus?" "My pleasure! My queen! Of course!" *She smiles!*

Tamesh moves from the couch to one of two caned queen chairs on the balcony. There's a magnificent view of the mountain from there. Doe hands her the refilled glass *she'd refreshed her own* and takes the chair next to her. They sit in silence watching *her* tears fall and listening to the rumblings of *her* protests!

Nate looks about smiling and nodding his head as he enters Bahi's chamber. "You've made some v-e-r-y nice changes!" he comments moving to the bar. *Bahi gives a brief smile!* "I'm glad you like it!" Nate grabs a bottle of 'IMOYA' (South African brandy) off of the shelf, two glasses and returns to where he sits. He places the glasses on a small table and pours each half full. *Bahi picks up his glass, takes a sip and his eyes narrow to him.* "What's the problem, my son? What's going on?" *He lowers his head a bit.* "It's Doe and me too, I guess! I feel as she! *He raises his head.* Bahi! We never thoroughly understood the requirement of duty. We'd no idea nor thought that it was to witness and record the unending assault, destruction, misery, pain and violation of *her*, day in day out, year upon year, century after century compounded with that of *her daughters* and *their off-spring!* It's maddening and becoming increasingly more unbearable! Right now she wants to--!" Mobahi cuts his words, "I'll not hear of it! We'll not hear of it! You just... you both just need some R&R! It's good you're home! Son, we've all missed the two of you! Even though Doe visits more often than you, we enjoy both of you best when together! You'll see! Once they (*those of the village*) know you're at home, you won't have any peace!" he jests. But his attempt at joviality isn't fooling Nate! He feels unrest within him! "*What's it Bahi? What aren't you telling me?*" *He gives a heavy sigh and casts his eyes downward for a moment.* "Son, there's a whispering of early evacuation and that command's strongly considering recalling all of us! If it's true that indicates something's occurring to *Earth* that we're unaware of!" "Bahi! That's doubtful! Our reports of *her* have been meticulous and observations thoroughly executed!" "You're right son! It must be information known only to higher command! Just thought you should be aware!"

They're administered calming therapies and pampered for the next three days. They inspect the various facilities and visit the village as discussed. By the fifth day they're balanced, their focus and spirit's been restored. In two days they'll depart for 'Angel Place'.

CHAPTER THREE
candidates

APRIL 24TH
Fairfield, California

Menacing winds whip thru the air as torrential bullets fall relentlessly from the smoky gray sky. *'It's uncommonly cold for this time of year! It used to be warmer! And still there're those who rebuff the reality of climate change! Why'd it have to rain today? Of all days!'* Races thru her mind as she pulls into the parking lot. She desires everything to be as perfect as possible for their coveted appointment with the co-chair of the 'Foundation'. A philanthropic group financed by the 'Greenwood Corporation' known to target and assist women with humanitarian efforts, but also others who've sound business plans or inventions with operational capital and essential support after they've been denied by traditional institutions. Today, she and Janet are presenting a plan designed to eradicate economic poverty and address mental illness in low-income areas.

Claire Tamarumaro opens the car door, gathers her briefcase and hits the release button on the handle of her umbrella! It springs open, she sprints to the office door, steps thru, quickly lowers the umbrella and slips it into the receptacle. But not fast enough to avoid creating a path of water beads. "A real mess out there huh?" comments Lauren (office manager) peering up from her station. "That's an understatement!" she snarls clearly agitated as she wrestles out of her raincoat. "Is he here?" "Yes. They're in the conference room." "Thanks! Uhh…tell me? How do I look?" "Relax…relax! You look fine! Take a deep breath and exhale. Now go in there and get it done! I'm counting on everything working out so I can get a long over-due raise!" "Good luck with that!" Claire chuckles, empathetically patting the ledge of her work station as she passes by! *The new model, fully loaded, Jaguar in the parking lot belonged to Lauren and it was paid for!*

Jae's standing at the rear of the room, next to the service, chatting with a well-dressed man whose face Claire cannot see as she enters. But she'd detected a seductive fragrance in the hallway that could only belong to him! Jae excuses herself and moves swiftly to her, "Girl! You're right on time! I was running out of conversation!" Jae's obviously nervous and Claire's taken aback! She's rarely seen her rattled! She looks into her face inspective, "Are you alright? Something wrong?" Jae shakes her head while gently cupping her elbow, "No. Nothing's wrong! That's the problem! Come on!" He smiles and extends his hand as they near, "Hello! Ms. Tamarumaro. It's a pleasure to meet you! I'm Michael Fenfox. I'm hoping you'll call me, Michael. Your associate speaks very highly of you! As a matter of fact, you've been the center of conversation since my arrival!" *She shoots a darting glance to Jae! Jae averts her eyes!* "The pleasure's mine! I assure you and please call me Claire! It's easier. Although, surprisingly you pronounced it correctly! You know Michael? She really gets to me with that! She's really the gifted one! But what can I do? She's my best friend, my sister and colleague!" He chuckles lightly! *'How extraordinary!' he ponders in amazement of their friendship, humility and love! They're spiritually gorgeous! Absolutely beautiful!'* "Well, let's get started!" Claire invites. They seat themselves, the lights of the room dim and their presentation begins.

Forty-five minutes later,

The lights return and he rises from his seat applauding! "That was amazing! You've formulated a well-designed strategy! Quite aggressive and highly innovative! Very much in line with the mission of the 'Foundation'! I'm submitting my recommendation to the 'Chair' right away! Hopefully, we can get your project underway within…uh, say six weeks! You know! I think it's only fitting that we christen our new alliance over dinner! Will you join me at 'Garvey's' this evening? Say 7:30?" His approving words and invitation paralyzes both with shock! Claire recovers first. "That's very generous of you! We'd be delighted!" "This will be a treat for me! I'll send for you if you'll provide your addresses." Claire scribbles on the back of a business card and hands it to him. He places it inside his breast pocket, rises from the table and begins donning his raincoat, "I'm looking forward to this evening! Thank-you ladies and good-day!" Jae still hasn't said a word since he mentioned 'Garvey's'. *Its an eight star rated restaurant patronized by the rich, prominent, famous and the common man, on special occasions! It's nearly impossible to get a reservation! Both had been there once for a charity event unaccompanied!*

They eye each other and pinch as a reality check! "Claire did you hear what he said?" A broad smile crosses her face, "G-i-r-l! Yes, I heard! We heard! He not only gave us an unofficial thumbs up! He's taking us to Garvey's and sending a car! I'm closing the office early. I'll be home after three." exclaims Jae. "That sounds good! I'll call you when I get home!" Claire grabs her briefcase, hurries to the reception area and quickly dons her raincoat. Lauren notices her rush, "Is something wrong?" "Ask Jae!" she replies snatching her umbrella and stepping thru the door into the rain. Lauren leaves her station and taps on her door frame, "What's going on?" In a faux snobbish British accent Jae replies, "Michael Fenfox has approved our project, invited us to dine at 'Garvey's' tonight and sending a car!" "Shut the front door! Do y'all need some back-up?" "N-o-o! We're big girls!" Jae returns laughing! Lauren smiles deep within herself! It'd been a good while since she'd seen her bubbly and even longer since she'd heard heartiness in her laughter!

Jae finalizes the last matter demanding her attention a little after 2:30 p.m. She notices four lights pulsating on her communication unit. The first three are confirmations for future consults. The last is a Dr. Oka. His name's not familiar. He'd left his number and requested a return call at her earliest convenience. She jots down the number and dials, but receives no answer. She gathers her things and heads home.

At 6:30 p.m. Claire's intercom buzzes. It's Mr. Jeffrey, the guard at the front gate, alerting her to the vehicle's arrival. She thanks him, grabs her purse and takes a last glance into the mirror. The sensors of the double-doors detect her approach and open revealing a handsome, smiling, well-dressed chauffeur awaiting her. "Good-evening, Ms. Tamarumaro! I'm Byron." he greets offering his arm. "Good-evening!" she returns accepting and smiling! *She's stunned he'd pronounced her name correctly and by the vehicle that awaits at the curb!* The rear passenger door of the titanium colored Rolls Royce 'Ghost' with translucent tires and purple water rims stands open. She eases in.

A group of teenagers are playing hoops in a driveway, residents are pruning flowers, others are mowing their lawns and a group of men are engaged in sidewalk conversation as the stately 'Ghost' glides onto Bamboo Drive and parks in front of her residence. The lawnmowers quiet, all conversations cease and eyes shift! Even for this upscale community it's a rarely seen vehicle that reeks wealth. Byron steps out and proceeds to her door! Eye-popping physique and immaculately dressed he's more than easy on the eyes and all are on him! He presses the doorbell. Within seconds it opens. *He's stunned by her! And she too by him!* "Good-evening, Ms. Janet! I'm Byron. All set?" "Ye-Yeh-Yes!" she stutters! He offers his arm and escorts her while being eyed by the envious women, drooling, dirty old men and testosterone driven young boys of the neighborhood! Hell! She's blazing! Together they're flaming! Claire watches as they seemingly glide to the car and she eases in, "Uh! Jae? You in heat? G-i-r-l! You're beggin! Just n-a-s-t-y!" "Uhh...aah...um people who live in glass houses shouldn't throw stones! Plus! It's the Ivory effect!" *They giggle!* Byron presses a button and the tinted glass-like partition begins to part from its center and fold into the sides of the interior fan-like as if made of paper. "Excuse me! But you must be v-e-r-y special! I've been his driver for a good while, rarely have I carried any ladies and never socially! The roses and champagne are for you! His compliments! So please! Enjoy and have a wonderful evening!" he bids in a sexy tenor, British accented voice. Resting on the white marble counter

25

in front of them are two long stemmed, hybrid red/black roses, a highly polished sterling silver ice bucket containing a magnum of '1970 Mondavi (2K a bottle) champagne and two 'Waters Edge' crystal flutes with the date and their names etched on them! They look to each other and smile! "Girl! We, I could get use to this!" Jae comments giddily! "Ya think? Now will you please pop the cork and pour!" begs Claire. "Okay! I hope it helps to calm our butterflies! 'Cause mine are fluttering like crazy!"

The 'Ghost' turns onto the wide horse shoe driveway at 7:58 p.m. It comes to a halt between two thirty foot high granite statues of Queen Asheba and King Tutankhamen inscribed with aged hieroglyphics that look authentic! Two handsome, finely attired, armed guards are posted at the entrance, a forty foot high, twenty feet wide double-door of middle Eastern influence made of ebony and shittim (*acadia*) both rare woods. The door's rumored to be 6,000 years old! *The owner refuses its testing!*

They recognize the 'Ghost' and vacate their posts to greet its passengers. The first opens the door and assists Jae, the second assists Claire. They escort them thru the ancient doors, down a red carpeted vestibule into an ornate parlor where they're met by a handsome genie wearing a silk and leather, gold embroidered vest that highlights his chiseled arms and eight-pack abs! A blinding white turban rests upon his rounded bald head accented by a gold medallion encrusted with blue diamonds at its center. He seats them in throne chairs, replaces their footwear with bejeweled silk slippers then escorts them to the 'Olive Tree'. All eyes turn as they enter and Michael's speechless! They look like models! Nothing like the traditionally attired business women he'd encountered earlier! After a few cocktails and introductions to celebrities, athletes and politicians Malik informs that their feasting chamber's ready. Before the trio can get out of the lounge he's approached by a few associates. They probe him for information concerning the ladies! This is the first time they've ever seen him with any socially! He says not a word, but smiles!

His eyes twinkle as he looks to them during dessert. "Thank-you for such a marvelous evening! I haven't had this much fun in a very long time. I've missed this! Oh! Please forgive me for not complimenting you until now! But you had me all twisted up as you walked into the lounge! The two of you were...are just gorgeous!" *Jae and Claire chuckle!* "Thank-you! Michael this has been such an enchanting evening and the meal was scrumptious! However, you made our eyes pop too!" states Jae flirtatiously. "Yes! Michael! This has been v-e-r-y nice! Thank-you!" adds Claire. He glances at the time...10:12 p.m. "Uh...oh! It's time I got you ladies home!" They gather themselves and exit. As they're walking out Jae murmurs to Claire, "I've got to pick Ivory up at the airport in the morning! I hope I don't over sleep!" "Don't worry I've got your back!" "Yeah? Well, who's got yours?" They load into the 'Ghost'.

Byron glances into the rearview mirror as he merges onto the expressway and smiles! His passengers have drifted off to sleep! Jae's head's resting on Michael's shoulder and he and Claire lean on each other. He's never seen him so peaceful! Turning into Jae's driveway he announces, "Uh...sir! Sir!" Michael stirs. Jae and Claire awake. Michael escorts each to their door, checks inside and out to ensure their safety and thanks each once more for a great evening!

He's too excited to sleep when he returns to the corporate penthouse! He'd *felt* something from them as he had the other two! Prospects are very high that one of them is who they seek! He can't wait 'til morning! He grabs the 'cd' and presses Jonas Matthis number and informs him of what's occurred, what he needs and provides their addresses. Next he calls Nate! Jonas *alerts the 'keepers!*

Jae and Claire were both college freshman attending different schools when they met during a 'FEC' Feminine Empowerment Conference' in Las Vegas. Their friendship grew rapidly. They've shared their deepest secrets, fears, hopes, dreams, nightmares and have become integral parts of each other. They're BSFs! (Best Sister Friend)

CHAPTER FOUR
ivory's arrival

APRIL 25TH
5:00 a.m.

The sun's just awakening as the alarm blares and the phone rings! In one swift movement she turns off the alarm and answers, "Claire?" "Hey girl! Yes, it's me! Time to rise and shine!" "Okay! Okay! Claire. I'm up! Thank-you! I'll call you later." She terminates the call, springs from the bed, goes to the kitchen and turns on the coffee maker. Then rushes into the bathroom for the morning rituals. By 6:25 a.m. groomed, dressed and ready to take on the world she's about to prepare that first cup when the doorbell rings! She turns off the coffee maker, gathers her things, scampers down the walkway and climbs into the taxi.

It pulls up to the curb of the arrival terminal at 7:35 a.m. She pays her then makes her way to the TransGlobal concourse, gate #8. Ivory's flight's just disembarking. After a few minutes she spots her engaged in conversation with a very, exotic man as they emerge from the airplane's accordion tunnel into the spacious arrival area! He's eye-catchingly handsome! Ivory sees her, waves and indicates to him that she's the friend she'd been speaking of!

They meet midway and give each other warm, 'sisterly' hugs! Ivory introduces, "Janet Xuan Shang-Brooks, this is Chikoya Oka. Ah, excuse me! I mean Dr. Oka." Smiling he extends his hand, "It's my pleasure to meet you! Ivory speaks very highly of you! And please! Call me Ko." Jae returns his smile and gives Ivory the *look* as he gently shakes her hand. *His hands are baby soft!* "She's a tendency to exaggerate, poor dear! She means well though! And please, call me Jae!" *He chuckles! 'These two are really some-thing!'* "I don't know her that well yet! But I seriously doubt any exaggeration! Listen? Can I persuade the two of you to join me for dinner?" "That's very kind of you, but I'm tied up this evening! Tomorrow evening would be better!" Ivory replies. "Good! Then it's a date! May I have your number so that I can provide you the details later?" "Of course!" Ivory takes a personal, not professional, card from her planner and hands it to him. "Fine. I look forward to tomorrow evening!" *As he walks away the name Shang-Brooks rings familiar to him! But he's unable to place it!*

Jae eyes her as they continue to the exit. "He's charming, intelligent, handsome and a doctor! Hmm, I must say he's n-i-c-e! You always find prime fruit! How do you do it? What's your mojo? Oh! Do you have any baggage?" "No. I'm trying a new baggage service in the wake of so many horror stories of theft and lost. They'll arrive at your office. When I'm ready to continue travel I just call and confirm the new pick-up location and destination. To answer the other part of your question (she pauses and gestures a sassy slip of her hips and a swivel of her head). Now come on! Stop playing! You know the 'mojo' is me! After all, am I not amazing?" "Girl, please!" *They chuckle.* "It does sound like a smart idea! Ivory, I think I'll try it!" A taxi pulls to the curb where they stand and the driver leans over to the open passenger window, "Good-morning ladies! Need a ride?"

"Yes." they reply. He hops out and opens their door. "Any luggage?" "No." Before pulling off Jae gives him two addresses, her office and residence. She pays him more than enough to cover both fares and a generous tip. They resume their conversation. "Now! Back to Dr. Oka!" Jae urges. "Oh! Okay! So, as I enter the cabin there's a noticeable stench! Its source's an extremely obese man occupying a window and the middle seat. The aisle seat's empty and it's the one indicated on my ticket! *Unbeknownst to the passengers and crew the man suffered with trimethylaminuria. His body's unable to break down the chemical compound that causes him to have a pungent odor.* I started looking about for an empty seat and noticed the doctor seated next to the window, six rows back, on the opposite side of the plane. He'd placed his laptop in the seat next to him, but the aisle seat was empty! Fortunately, the flight hadn't sold out! So I asked if he'd mind me sitting there. He smiled no objection. He'd gotten a whiff of the reason for my request! After that we introduced ourselves and began small talk!" Executing a defiant eye roll Jae fires back, "Oh! So! I'm small talk now?" Their conversation's cut short by arrival to her office. "The tank's full. I'll see you later!" Jae informs climbing out. *Ivory's in town for two reasons: first to visit with Jae. Secondly, to fulfill a request to be the keynote speaker at the Archaeological Symposium on Saturday. Presently, she's the world leading expert. Jae will be her plus one! Ivory has her own set of keys and knows her security codes.*

"Good-morning Jae! *Lauren greets as she enters the office. Only in the public eye does she refer to her formally.* Hmmph! Girl! You've got a glow! What's up? How *good* was *last night?" Jae smiles mischievously!* "Last night was a fantasy fulfilled! Lauren, the food was s-o-o good, the service off the chart and the ambience amazing! The entire establishment reeks of 'old world' Middle Eastern décor reminiscent of 'Arabian Nights'! Claire and I were given authentic bejeweled harem slippers as souvenirs! It was a wonderful experience! Guess who he introduced us to?" she teases heading to her office. "Stop teasing and tell!" snaps Lauren following behind. "Okay! But you might want to sit down first!" Jae starts reciting names, "Sylar Perri, Monna Brasil, Mon Hovi, Angel Julie, Conrad Pitman, Barber Myzand and Goldman Whoola! It was surreal! Michael's very charming, handsome and brilliant! It's a bit scary to see all the attributes any woman could desire wrapped in one fine package!" "Oh! So it's Michael now! I'm glad y'all had a nice time! Does he have any brothers?" "Oh! Speaking of packages, I hope you get a chance to see the hunk that Ivory met on her flight! I swear Mother Nature's chest truly has a gaping hole! *She remembers Ivory's luggage.* Uhh? Have Ivory's bags been delivered?" "Yes! They're in the conference room." "Good! But seriously you've got to experience Garvey's if I have to take you myself! I'll ask Michael to arrange a reservation for us." "Now that sounds like a plan!" smiles Lauren moving toward the door. The extension lights glow and pulsate erratically! Jae looks to her, "Our public's calling!"

Ivory calls Jae a little after 2 p.m. "Hey girl! Everything alright there?" "Oh sure, Jae! I just wanted to know if we're eating out?" "Now Ivory! You know full well how I feel about your cuisine! There's not a chef that out-shines you!" *Ivory giggles!* "Hmm, hmp! You sure know how to flatter! Okay! I'll whip something up!" "Hey! Wait a minute! Aren't we having din-ner with your friend?" "No. That's tomorrow night! I'll tell you about that when you get home!" "Oh! Okay! Hey! Would you please put *that* bottle of champagne on ice?" *Ivory pauses.* "Uhh…sure! But isn't *that* bottle very special to you? You sure?" "O-o-h yes! I'll explain later!" Their call ends. Jae's voice and tone had been high spirited! A sound Ivory hasn't heard in a long time, but's delighted to hear! She'll prepare something special for whatever she's celebrating! Ivory grabs her purse, keys, climbs into the vin-tage mint condition, canary yellow 1972 white convertible GTO and heads out to the markets! Top down of course! *Due to her frequent visits all the merchants in the area and local police know her and the vehicle! She's never received a ticket! Only un-announced visits, dinner invitations and flowers!* After ending their call Jae recalls the message and the name…Oka. *She ponders, 'If he's the same person she's just met?'* She removes the headset and turns off the computer. Ecstatic from the success of the day she closes the law offices early for a long-weekend and announces double-time pay for the catering staff and employees working the week-end!

The phone rings at 3:30 p.m. It's the dispatcher alerting her that the taxi's outside. She goes to the door and gestures the driver inside for the bags. After a last minute inspection she arms the alarms, secures the door and climbs into the cab. Next stop, 2568 Bamboo Drive, Hacienda Heights, California…home. *A suburb southeast of Fairfield.*

It's 4:38 p.m. when the driver sets the last bag in the garage. She's met by intoxicating aromas wafting thru the air as she climbs the steps. Ivory's at the kitchen counter pouring a goblet of wine when she enters. She surveys the space and gives her the *look!* "What? What?" challenges Ivory hunching her shoulders! "Did you cook?" *Ivory's looking at her as if she's ten heads!* "Of course! Why're we having this conversation?" "Because it's super clean in here!" *Ivory chuckles!* "Now Jae! You know I can't stand mess!" "Oh, yeah! How'd I forget that?" *Ivory rolls her eyes*! "Jae! Go and unwind! You really need it! Then you can tell me about this great new thing…uh…*man!*" The word *man* causes her to momentarily freeze! Then it dawns on her! *Ivory thinks it's a man who's the cause of her joy!* "Uhhh…okay!" she replies lifting Ivory's glass from the counter en route to her room. "Oh! Your luggage's in the garage." "Thanks, Jae!"

She emerges minutes later visibly refreshed! "N-o-w! You look like you! Come! I'm dying to hear your great news!" Jae's about to seat herself when she glimpses something from the corner of her eye in the dining room. They widen as she approaches speechless!

Ten piece pewter service for two, linen dinner napkins, her finest china, crystal flutes and water glasses! In the center of the table a beautiful arrangement of white roses, baby's breath, rare dwarfed Birds of Paradise and fragrant candles alit are placed about! "Ivory! The table's absolutely amazing! What time's your guest arriving?" Ivory nearly chokes on the sip she's taking! "W-h-o-a! Whoa! Calm down! That's for us! We're **celebrating** something…right?" An overwhelming feeling of emotion washes over Jae and her eyes well! "You did all of this for me?" "Jae! Come on! It's nothing for me to cook! What's-?" She interrupts, "Yeah-yah Ivory! And we normally eat off of everyday plates, there're no exotic flowers, candle sticks nor fine china!" "Well! You sounded so happy I just wanted to make it special! I'm pleased that you like it!" "I'm sorry! Thank-you!" Jae offers with an apologetic smile. *Ivory's eyebrow arches* "Now tell me? What's made you so happy?" *She glances toward the ceiling as if receiving instructions and plops down on the sofa beside her.* "Remember me telling you about the 'Foundation' and Michael Fenfox? *She nods.* "Well! He's recommending Claire and I be granted the funding! That's the first part of my good news. The second' part's that I closed on three contracts today with the

Cordero Winery, Americas Golf Association and the Medical Suppliers Corporation! Each awarded a million dollar signing bonus!" A look of pride spreads across Ivory's face! "Jae! Those are some of the wealthiest business entities in the country!" She reaches for her hands and squeezes them gently, "Congratulations! Very nice! You go girl! I told you something like this would happen for you! You're excellent at what you do!" Jae releases from her grasps and hugs her impulsively, "Yes! You did! You never lost faith in me! I love you my friend! Thank-you!" Ivory gently begins trying to pry away from her, "Alright! Come on! Let me go now! You know we don't swing like that!" Ignoring Ivory's protest wriggling she continues, "Ivory? Know what the best part is?" "No Jae! What?" she replies clearly frustrated and still struggling! "It's that between the Foundation's funding and the bonuses I'll be able to hire additional employees and offer a good living wage with benefits!" Finally free from her Ivory stands, nods and exhales deeply, "Now! I completely understand why we're uncorking *this* bottle!" She pops the cork, pours and they raise their flutes. Ivory toasts, "To my best, charming, intelligent and gentle friend!" They tap. *Ping!* "Hmmm... this was a very good year! Can we eat now? I'm starved!" begs Jae. "Sure. I'm hungry too!" chimes Ivory. "Hey? What happened to our future dinner date?" Jae queries. "Oh! He called with a very sincere apology! Seems family business will have him tied up. Hmp! I was looking forward to learning more about him!" "Girl, me too!" Ivory goes to the kitchen to begin warming the food and Jae turns on the monitor. A breaking news alert streams across the bottom of the screen. Ivory notices it too returning into the room. The visual's a man being escorted from the posh 'Oasis' hotel by two secret servicemen to a waiting government motorcade with a Californias State Highway police escort at its front and rear. The video's from earlier that day and time stamped...10:40 a.m. PST, local time.

Jae looks to Ivory, "Doesn't he look kind of familiar?" As they're about to strain for more focus a close-up image appears. The text box displays, 'Dr. Chikoya Oka, gifted, world renowned, neural surgeon has been summoned to St. Andrews Hospital to attend to Senator Dowland of New

York who was attending the International Ecological Summit and suffered a myocardial infraction. Dr. Oka was in the region for a tribal council.' Jae and Ivory look to each other dumbfounded! *Who knew?* The doorbell rings. It's his deliveries!

CHAPTER FIVE
inðian naȼion

APRIL 25TH
7:50 a.m. PST

When he passes thru the double-doors into the light of day he's met by an alluring woman with dancing light eyes, silky dark hair and a body built by nature! She moves to him and hugs him tenderly, "Ko! We're so glad you've come!" He pauses and gives her a questioning stare, "Neemah? Did you doubt my presence? Did you really think I wouldn't come?" "No! No! I knew you'd come if you could! But I...we also know how busy you've been and how many require your gift!" They resume walking to the parking lot. "Yeah? Well, what's happening at the Center? Any new programs being implemented? How's the membership? Has the local law enforcement been harassing our people?" She pauses and throws her hands up feigning surrender, "Whoa! Whoa! Please calm yourself! A meeting's been called by the Elders this afternoon. Hopefully, you'll find your answers there!"

They load into her vehicle and exit the lot. *Her voice fills with emotion as the ride.* "Ko! So much has gone wrong and is wrong for our people, especially our young! Just as we were reaching the brink of possibility for equality, unity, real upward mobility and peace, out of nowhere intentional 'man-made' obstacles appear and destroy our progress! Our future's being slaughtered just like the black ones and others of coloration!" There's shared silence between them.

She hands him her card as they pull up to the entrance of the 'Oasis' at 8:46 a.m. He glances at it, turns and stretches his arm to the backseat and grabs his bags, "I need to take care of a few things before the meeting." "Of course! Call me! Use the first number." He nods, "Say around three?" "That'll be perfect!"

9:25 a.m.

After showering and thinking about the evening to come he realizes there'll be no time for the planned date tomorrow evening. He retrieves Ivory's card and dials her number. It rings a few times then he hears a soft sultry, "Hello?" "Hi Ivory!" She recognizes his voice immediately! "Oh! Hi, Ko! How's your day?" she inquires thoughtfully. "Very busy. But thanks for your concern! Ivory I never mentioned why I was in town during our conversation. But the truth's I'm here for two reasons. However, the main reason concerns family affairs and it's going to take more time than I'd planned. I'm afraid I need to ask for a rain check on dinner, if you'll give me one!" "Oh sure! Of course, you can have a rain check! That's not a problem. Is there anything we can do?" "How very generous of you, but no!" "Well, we'll catch-up when we can!" "Ivory, I really like the way you think! Thank-you so much for your understanding! You will hear from me dear lady! Um, Ivory? Would you mind giving me Jae's address?" She finds his request a bit odd, but honors it. His next call's to a florist. He orders two exotic floral arrangements. As an added measure of his regret he also orders fresh fruit baskets! As he ends the call there's a knock on the door! He opens it and is met by two clean shaven men wearing dark suits and brandishing badges.

3:00 p.m.

He's recharged, fragrant and very handsome in the turquoise shirt accented by chocolate linen trousers and leather moccasins when Neemah returns to the Oasis. She gets a whiff of him as he climbs in, "O-o-o-h! You smell wonderful!" she compliments. "Good! Now you know I'm a-l-l clean!" he jokes! "W-e-l-l?" she teases. *They laugh!* The sound of tribal rhythms play on the audio as she pulls off. *Her memory flashes back to the days of their youth when he'd be covered in dirt and mud from head to toe, a frog in his hands or tadpoles in a jar. She chuckles within!* "Hey! Saw you on the news. How long you been back?" "Oh, maybe an hour." "Do the powerful have you on speed dial?" *He chuckles.* "No! Not at all! They have to go thru the chief of staff and then he has to contact Nikki. She's the only one who always knows where I am and she's very scrutinizing!" She gives him a quick glance, "The two of you've been together for a long time! What five or six years? You telling me there's nothing either of you share other than work?" "Yes, Neemah! I know she's cute, sexy and brilliant! But she's extremely principled and disciplined! She's far superior to me and I've the good sense to realize it!" She nods understanding and queries, "Uh…back to the senator, how is he?" "Oh, he's out of danger. He'd suffered a cerebral aneurysm not a myocardial infraction as reported! He's in great health, that factor alone made it a simpler fix. Plus, St. Andrews had everything essential for the surgery."

They turn onto exit #13 of the interstate which leads to a neglected two lane highway. After a few miles they turn into the Wicatah reservation and travel its 'Broadway', a dirt road, for a quarter mile. When they arrive to the entrance gate it's unmanned! Federal guards are supposed to be posted! But on this day and obviously too many others they're absent and it's in freedom mode! As they proceed what he sees is appalling and gut-wrenching! Weather-worn, abused, collapsing shanties and discarded pets wander aimlessly. Young squaws prostituting, using and selling drugs, as well as young warriors (males 16-34 yrs.) The old ones look poorly, physically and spiritually! Neglected young ones dirty, barefooted, soiled, hungry and scantily clothed wander from shack to shack in search of their delinquent parent/s who're oblivious to their needs! Still others, young and old, gather at the drinking place in a vain attempt to drink their anguish, despair and hopelessness away! The mixing of the sexes is not a practice of tradition. Yet unmarried and under age females are pregnant! His heart aches and eyes well! He's seen enough! "I don't need to see anymore! Let's get to the meeting!" he requests clearly upset! She turns at the slight fork in the road that leads to the 'Great Hall'.

As they approach people are flooding into the meeting place and its parking area's full. These numbers haven't been witnessed in a very long time! If change had an identifying scent, it was in this place, at this time! He's quickly greeted by Big Cat at the entrance. *They'd met and become fast friends during the summer of his eleventh birthday and annual visit with his grandmother. Big Cat had always been the bigger kid of the group in physique. He was even bigger now! They're truly blood brothers!* "I realize much time has passed since we've shared each other's presence! Is all well for and with you?" Big Cat inquires. Ko looks to him and smiles, "I am well. And you? Your family?" "We're alright, little brother!" "Big Cat everything's so much worse for our people! Especially the young! Isn't it?" *He nods reluctantly.* "For a time all was going well, in a swift upward direction! Now there's nothing. Our lives as a Nation are at a standstill! Chaos rules." Big Cat states with an eerie sadness. He plants his hand firmly on Big Cat's shoulder, "Trust me! It's going to be corrected!" The trio continues to the Great Hall.

As soon as Ko enters his spirit's felt by all within! He's seated next to the eldest chief, Great Bear, around a huge oak conference table with a large calumet intricately carved at its center. Great Bear turns his head and eyes to him, "Many have left the reservation and traveled into the world of the 'light ones'. Few have returned whole, unaffected by their contact. But you! You've returned always and unaffected! You've never forgotten who and what you are! We need your guidance. Tell us what we need to do to save ourselves and our generations!" He glances first to Neemah. She gives an encouraging nod! Next he eyes Big Cat, who returns a stone cold warrior stare of courage and support! Only then does he rise. There's a strange quiet as he moves to the speaking spot. He looks about the room and exhales, "Neemah took me on a tour. Needless to say, I did not like what I saw! Too many of our people have digressed and again been defeated by the diversions placed before them! Also it doesn't help when so-called 'brothers' aid the 'light ones' for monetary gain! When the 'light ones' came to the shores of our land, we did not attack them and they were not the best and brightest! On the contrary we accepted and allowed them to share in the bounty of our land. We were then and remain a people of love, harmony, peace and unity! We aided in their survival! We posed no threat! And remember they bore no gifts. But they weren't empty handed! They brought fire water, incongruous diseases, strange weapons and naked evil! It's time to stand-up and wake-up! They're jeopardizing the extinction of 1,300 species presently! Time to begin our own resurrection. We cannot and will not let them harm *Mother Earth* any further! We must begin *her* healing as well as our own...ourselves! We must take our land back! A handful of 'light ones' have laid claim to 98% of our land! And still it's not enough! They want more of our sacred places! Their fate will be decided by the council and executed with compassion and mercy! Unlike the way they've treated our ancestors and others! Within the Nation we've teachers, lawyers, accountants, engineers, doctors, plumbers and electricians etc. They've been lured away from their heritage. It's time we got them back! *The sound of pounding feet's thunderous in the room!* We can move forward! Our ancestors never fathomed the depth of evil that dwelled inside the 'light ones' was so vile! But! This is a new day! It's time to awaken! It's time to reclaim our land! It's time for change! After all, it's the 'light ones' who've reneged on every treaty they've ever signed and slaughtered thousands of our people and others!" Great Bear interrupts, "We've been awaiting the 'Great Spirit'! We shall go forward with your vision!" *The sound of pounding feet fills the air once again! It's their applause!*

CHAPTER SIX
cɑnꝺiꝺɑꞇe ꝺɑꞇɑ submissions

APRIL 30TH

10:15 a.m.
Los Angeles, Californias

G uards at the gate of the corporate hanger of the Regis airport recognize the 'Ghost' as it speeds toward them and hoist the barricade. It flies thru and halts in front of the 'AP' hangar. Michael climbs out and boards the modified Dassault Falcon 6X. He gazes out the window as the craft ascends and ponders, *'Have I really found one?'* His submissions over the years have been fruitless despite his efforts! However, this time something feels different!

12:35 p.m.

Hurricane Mills, Tennessee

The Falcon descends onto the tarmac. He disembarks, climbs into the waiting vehicle and is delivered to the front entrance. Shane steps to the vehicle as it pulls to the curb. He's about to reach for the handle when the door opens and Michael steps out. "Hey, Shane!" His eyes widen in surprise and sparkle with adoring friendship as they shake hands and man-hug! His facial expression changes to suspicion and his eyebrows raise! "Are they expecting you?" Michael hangs his head. "No. I thought I'd surprise them!" *Shane exhales, touches a finger to his temple, nods contemplatively, smiles and comments,* "Hmmmm…you know? You may be just what they need!" Michael frowns confused by his words, "What do you mean?" "It hasn't only been blue around here! Lately, it's been fading

40

to gray! Oh! The businesses are fine! It's them! It's as if the ideology of love, the celebration of being, the joy and all it brings has vanished from them! They function. They do not live." "How long has this been-?" Shane interrupts, "Since you were here last!" *That'd been a little more than three years ago!* Michael exhales and gives him an eye wink! "Not to worry old friend! I'll do what I can!" He proceeds up the stairs, pauses on the landing and looks up. Unusual birds for this region of the world are flying leisurely to and fro! Some singing, others chattering! He lowers his gaze to survey the beauty of nature outstretched before him! Flowers bloomed and blooming, an assortment of manicured trees and grasses everywhere! There's such a feeling of peace in this place! It's Eden-like!

Moments later he's about to ring the bell when the door bursts open! Startled by his presence she reflexively clutches her chest! "O-o-h, I'm sorry! I didn't mean to scare you!" he begs chuckling at her reaction. *She begins mockingly beating on his chest!* "Ooh! Oh, you! You! Why didn't you warn us you were coming?" "I wanted to surprise both of you!" *Her voice softens.* "Well, I'd say mission accomplished on that! How good of you to come! He could use a pick me up. You just gave me mine! Now back to you! What're you hiding? You're glowing, dear boy!" she queries with a piercing stare and 'cat that ate the canary' smile! He sets his briefcase down, steps into her, wraps his arms snuggly around her waist, lifts her from her feet and spins around. *She inhales his fragrance.* "Hmm! Whatever you're wearing's very nice! You're so urbane!" *He chuckles!* "Why, thank-you! But you! You remain stunningly gorgeous, timeless and your scent's always sweet and seductive!" he compliments lowering her. "Let me see what you're sporting!" she demands. He strikes a mannequin pose. "Well?" She scans him, shakes her head approvingly and smiles, "You're so charming and handsome, too!" "Why thank-you! But to be honest! I felt both of you needed a break and me too!" "Michael, you've always been good medicine!" *He knew her well and something was amiss! He lowers his head to look directly into her eyes.* "Now! Tell me truly? How are you?" "Oh, I'm alright! As a matter of fact, I'm perfect now that you're here! Come! Come!" she urges interlocking arms with him and pulling him along.

She notices him inhaling deeply and holding his breath for measured moments before exhaling slowly as they walk along. "Something wrong?" He gives a brief shake of his head and chuckles, "Oh no! It's good! It's so clean, so crisp and the linen fragrance's fantastic!" *She smiles!* "Oh! THAT! Its Nate's doing! You're well aware how he abhors 'public air'! He's increased the oxygen levels all over the estate, the Greenwood, the sub-stations and even the stables! He's also created an oxygen nasal device that can be worn hands-free for thirty-two hours before replenishment. He wears it faithfully when attending events and meetings at facilities other than our own! He's one for you too! It's in his office." Footsteps away from the doorway of his office she places a finger to her lips...sssh! Michael plasters himself to the side of the wall out of sight while she taps on its molding. Nate glances up and beckons. Feigning a tone and facial expression of distress she walks in, seats herself before him and begins to lament, "Nate, I'm sorry to interrupt you, but I have a very big problem and need your help!" He gives a sympathetic glance, lays down his pen, rises and seats himself in the chair next to her, "Of course! Anything! How can I help?" *She looks into his eyes.* "Well! For starters, you could take care of the problem at the door!" *Michael's been inconspicuously watching her performance and trying his best to contain his laughter! She's such a drama queen!* Nate turns. His face lights up! He rises and bolts to him! They embrace as loving brothers! "It's great to see you! Michael, you're a wonderful surprise!" In the blink of an eye his joy turns to concern, "This is a good visit, eh? There's not a situation?" Michael shakes his head emphatically. "Oh no, Nate! No! I just wanted to see you and Doe! Any objections?" *They're silent.* "Good! Now you have an hour to wrap up last minute business, alert the staff to end their workday and all report to the 'Party Room'. I'm home for a few days and would like to catch up with my family! Understand? Oh! Nate! I do hope you've plans to mass produce your device! I can't wait to try mine out! The air quality's deteriorating with each passing day! Now, if you'll excuse me I need to speak with the

42

kitchen." (Jamie, Petra and Maxx) *They look to each other and hunch their shoulders in defeat and compliance! The boss is home!* The kitchen trio are cuisine wizards extraordinaire with matching credentials! Oddly, each had found their passion for food in the kitchens of their grandparents at very young ages!

Jamie- Chef de Cuisine- is a product of the Le Cordon Bleu, Paris; Castello di Vicarello, Tuscany and the Culinary Arts Academy, Switzerland.

Maxx- Chef de Partie- is a product of Le Cordon Bleu, Paris; School of Artisan Food, UK; Pacific Institute of Culinary Arts, Canada and Culinary Arts Academy, Switzerland.

Petra-Executive/sous chef- is a product of Le Cordon Bleu, Paris; Ozeki Cooking School, Japan; New England Culinary Institute, Montepelier and Gastgewerbefachschule, Austria.

All invitees attend as requested, including security personnel, after activating additional surveillance systems. It's amazing what the kitchen prepares on such short notice! They have fun and carry on non-stop until a little after 9 p.m. when the last non-resident leaves.

Their heads rest against the back of the modestly stuffed, white leather sectional and their feet on ottomans. They're suffering from more than party fatigue! During the course of the evening Michael had detected the weakness of their 'LES' and taken notice of their oculi. They'd acquired a rust coloring, a verifying symptom of 'Nahzee'! "Okay, I want the truth! Have you been resting?" *They share looks of undeniable guilt!* "No! We haven't! Not really!" Nate confesses. *Michael sighs heavily, but's careful not to scold! Excitement's not helpful at this moment and would only exacerbate their condition.* "Well, that's not good! Grant would you please order assisted 'nahaea' baths drawn asap?" he requests calmly. Grant's nods acknowledgment. He reaches for his device and issues the orders! Meanwhile, Michael assists Doe and nudges Nate's feet causing him to rouse. Grant assists him.

After they've been put to rest Michael and Grant leave each of them at peace in their rooms respectively and enter the corridor. *Michael exhales.*

"Grant! Thanks for your help!" "No problem, Michael! It's good what you've done! They listen to you! And it's wonderful to have you home!" Michael gestures a back-hand wave as he heads to his suite. *Fortunately sleep and quiet's the cure! But they must adhere to a proper resting regiment going forward. Even they've a required minimum of fourteen hours per week for proper rejuvenation! He'd been tutored well by the 'keepers' regarding their care.*

Grant Dorkoff's the executive in charge of the estate's operations. All department heads report directly to him. His authority's superseded only by Doe and Nate and to date they've never challenged his decisions. He'd been recruited to be their guardian by their Uncle Kaseem when they were quite young. He's part of the family!

May 1st

Thunder claps, lightning flashes and rain pours from the early morning sky. Despite the clamor the trio sleep peacefully!

Grant diverts from his routine and heads to the 'Atrium' to greet and inform them of the activities he's planned for them. When he arrives the space's empty. He checks the time…8:51 a.m. *He ponders, 'They're probably in the Morning Room'.* But when he arrives there it's not only empty, but the service is undisturbed! A clear indication they're not up! He knocks lightly on Michael's door several times before he answers groggily, "Yes!" "Michael! It's me!" Grant calls softly. "Oh! Come in!" Grant steps in and looks him over measuredly, "You alright? Do you know what time it is?" "Uh…6:30?" "No Michael, try 9:08." "I guess I was more wiped out than I realized! Please give me a minute!" "Oh! No, no, no! No rush. You've company!" "You mean?" Grant nods, "Yes, them too!"

10:30 a.m.

Grant's watching the sea life within the aquarium, inset in the east wall, swim to and fro while sipping his favorite breakfast cocktail (mango & carrot juice) when they enter. "Good-afternoon! Glad you could make it! Everyone feel alright? Any complaints?" he queries with heavy sarcasm! *They look to each other like guilty children! Sarcasm was something Grant expressed only when he was extremely happy! They nod negatively to each other. This was not good! He's up to something!* As they select assorted pastries, fresh fruits, beverages of choice and seat themselves he rises and returns his empty glass to the cart. "Please! Excuse me! But some of us have tasks that must be attended! However, I've arranged for your favorite activities! We'll be waiting in the 'Atrium' when you're done! Dinner's at 7:00 and dress is casual elegant." he announces as he exits. They're puzzled! What activities? Who's the 'we'?

After satisfying their hunger and thirst they head for the Atrium and pause at the landing before descending. They see the mysterious *we* awaiting them below. Three instructors, aerobics, tai chi and weight lifting! *His idea of welcome home's a fifty minute aerobic work-out, forty-five minute weight session, massages, one hour spa services ending with pedicures and manicures!* They look to each other and whisper his name, *under their breath in unison,* as they reluctantly descend. *He's watching their reaction via in-house surveillance and laughing heartily!*

Four and a half hours later...

A healthy, average humanoid (29-43 yrs.) would've required the assistance of paramedics to resuscitate him or her from the work-out they've completed! But these **humans** are barely winded!

Later that evening...

Doe descends the staircase minutes after 7 p.m. and enters the 'Atrium'. *She pauses at the sight of the room. It's been transformed!* "Whoa! My word! You're absolutely stunning!" Nate exclaims as he enters from behind her. She'd been so absorbed with the sights surrounding her she'd not heard his footfalls. He's dressed to the casual nines. She turns to him, "Oh! You should talk! Wait! Wait! You **are** Nate? Right?" *He shakes his head!* "Ooh, no you don't! Don't change the subject! Doe! You're blazing! What's up? Is this for Michael?" "No! There's nothing between us! How many times do I have to keep telling you? Ask him?" "Ask who what?" Michael inquires having overheard the tail end of the conversation. Startled by his presence Nate quickly averts, "Ask you about today?" *He nods.* "Aah…the work-outs! Well, we know he's got a real weird way of showing affection!" "No stuff!" Doe remarks. As they laugh they hear the sound of someone clearing their throat! It's Grant! He moves from the shadowed corner where he's been since her arrival! They're stunned at the sight of him! He'd been very specific earlier regarding the dress code for dinner…casual elegant. But he's attired evening elegant! Spit-shined wing tips, charcoal gray, three piece, six button double breasted silk suit with matching vest, lavender shirt and white tie with lavender specks! He's always dapper, but this was over the top! They're speechless!

He moves to her smiling and offers his arm, "Shall we dine gorgeous?" After taking a few steps he pauses and glances over his shoulder, "You guys coming?" Michael and Nate look to each other dumbfounded for a second! Then follow. The banquet table's been replaced by a smaller one to accommodate the four and elegantly set with a candelabra ablaze gracing its midst. Grant guides her to the table, seats her and takes the chair to her left. The guys seat themselves. A caviar and shrimp appetizer graces each setting. Placed closest to Grant's a crystal stand bearing a matching ice bucket containing a magnum of champagne. He uncorks it, pours her glass, the others and his own. "This is a very special occasion for me! Because it's been quite a while since we've been together like this! At leisure with nothing pressing to resolve! It's the reason for my attire! It's in honor and celebration of you!" he toasts raising his flute in the air!

His words touch them deeply! They understand it's his way of expressing adoration! Overwhelmed they shake their heads and chuckle to mask their emotions! Michael gives him a piercing stare and feigns anger, "You told them to kill us didn't you?" *Referring to the work-outs! They erupt into laughter! Grant puts a finger to his temple gesturing air circles and shaking his head sympathetically.* "See! There really is something wrong with that one! He's loco! Come on! Let's dine!"

A twelve foot banquet table sits to their left against the wall. Steam from the highly polished silver chafing dishes curls in the air. They're laden with a lavish buffet of escargot, lobsters, lump crab meat cakes, salmon, Mahi-mahi, grouper, jasmine rice, asparagus and other delicacies! Red meat, chicken and pork are never on the menu. After sating their hunger they prepare dessert plates and return to the 'Morning Room'. Grant, Michael and Nate shed their jackets. Doe moves to the sofa, sits her plate on the coffee table, seats herself and removes her shoes.

Michael moves to the opposite end of the sofa and sits down inadvertently on the remote. Within seconds the monitors glow with images of the egotistical, maniacal, orange-haired COTA loudly boasting and lying about the size of his inauguration crowd, two years ago, for the millionth time! The biggest historical truth's that it was the smallest! "Sorry about that!" Michael offers scrambling to turn it off. Dora exhales, "I detest him and all those associated with him! The manner in which he treats *Earth* is beyond repulsive! Every time he kills one of Abamah's regulations to protect *her* it feels like someone pulling back the scab of a healing wound!" *There's silence.* Grant feels the weight of their empathy, "I know you're worried for *her.* But we must remain positive! *She* needs as much positive energy as possible to add with *her* own to sustain against their assaults. Of late *she's* been suffering historic events, fires, mudslides, quakes, volcanic eruptions, tsunamis and destructive storms. Theses manifestations are verifying factors of *her* attitude and condition! Their frequency, strength and duration are determinant of its increasing degree! *She* suffers from ERC caused by climate change inspired by the Bahleide and created by BT males thru their complete disregard and lack of respect for *her!* They're well aware of the damage and injuries they've caused and are causing! Yet despite the voices and physical demonstrations of protests and scientific evidence they continue to assault *her*! They hate *her greatness* and *her splendor*!" "Rotten bastards!" swears Nate. Grant gives him a disapproving glance and continues, "If only we could assist with the opening of their 'KSCs' and help them remember who and what they are! Collectively they've the remedy to ease *her* pain, discomfort and begin *her* healing! If awakened they'd also realize that presently the main source of evil upon *Earth* is the Russian and those like him! He's a ranking member in the 'Luminati. He's not a BT! He isn't even humanoid! He's the real deal! He's a Bahleide and has embedded his minions in various groups around the world thru all nations to sow seeds of chaos, hate and discord among those who desire the way of the Tauri, peace and harmony via lies, acts of treachery, murder and deceit! He's an evil genius and has delusions of ruling the world! One of the biggest lies they've successfully peddled is about *Earth!* Teaching *she's* inanimate! Which is a bold-faced lie! *She's* an extraordinary being, communicates and is very much alive! Presently, the star children and tribal Tauri in remote places are the only ones who still maintain the ability to communicate directly with *her* other than ourselves!" "Please excuse my use of profane words, but the ogre, Bahleide and BTs anger me!" Grant looks to him and the others silent for a moment, "Listen! I know the tasks are challenging! You've done well! But we must continue to hope that something will change. I'm going to turn in. *He looks to each with an endearing smile!* It's been a wonderful evening! Be well!"

May 2nd

8:34 a.m.

The Morning Room's their (Doe and Nate's) version of a breakfast/den combo. A place to gather their thoughts in the morning before descending to their offices. She's first to the room this morning and is pouring a chai latte as they enter. "How'd you beat us?" Michael challenges. "That's all I do!" she retorts! "Children! Children! Now, now! Let's play nice!" Nate interjects fatherly. *They laugh heartily!* "I'd forgotten how good it is when we're together! It's nice to wake-up to each other!" she comments. "I know!

48

Right?" chimes Michael. With child-like enthusiasm Nate queries "What're we going to do today?" Suddenly a ringing fills the room! They listen and scan intently, their ears directing their eyes! "It seems to be coming from the sofa!" says Doe moving toward it. She begins feeling in between the cushions and withdraws a still ringing 'cd'. It's Nate's! She hands it to him and he answers, "Good-morning!" On the opposite end Grant returns the greeting and begins informing him of his dilemma. After listening intently Nate replies, "Alright. I'll ask them and get back to you."

He looks to them with an expression they knew all too well! "What is it?" Michael queries. "One of our charities has an event for the children today! But three of the volunteers have cancelled. In essence they've three costumes that need bodies to fill them and Grant's asking us!" *They're silent for a moment.* Then she reminds, "Nate! You and I did a summer comedy workshop during our freshman and only year of study among BTs. Michael you know magic! Right? *He nods.* It sounds like fun! I'm in! I think we should do it!" she urges enthusiastically! "Me too!" says Michael. Nate sighs, "Well, it's unanimous!" While Nate's on the phone with Grant, Michael rises and turns to her, "I've got to make a call. I'll be right back!" He goes to his room and calls Jacques Denoir's *(a master magician)* number. He happens to be in Murfreesboro visiting his sister and answers. He's delighted to hear Michael's voice! They're old friends. Michael informs him of his need. "See you around 10!" says Jacques. *He'll bring a few props, but mostly he'll coach him.* He returns to the 'Morning' room and announces Jacques' arrival! *He doesn't tell them that he's paid Jacques to hire face painters to add to the children's entertainment!*

Shortly before eleven Michael thanks Jacques for his help, bids him farewell and closes the door. As he turns Grant seems to appear out of nowhere before him! "Are you ready?" he challenges frantically! "O-o-h yes!" Nervously Grant looks about, "Where are they? Aren't they ready? We've got to get a move on! The event begins at 1:00! " he barks. Michael smiles, "Calm yourself. I'll get them. We'll meet here in ten."

49

As promised they await him as he rushes toward them from the west wing corridor, "Come on! The car's waiting!" he snaps excitedly whizzing pass them! It's only after they've pulled out of the driveway and headed east onto Route #64 that he informs them of the schedule of events. The one detail he deliberately fails to mention is the identities of the mascots they'll be wearing!

They arrive to the Aurora Children's Center in suburban Chattanooga at 12:45 p.m. *It's a facility similar to Philadelphia's Children's Hospital, St. Jude's or the Shriner's in mission, scope and goals.* They locate the prep area and a volunteer directs them to their table. As they approach it they immediately begin shaking with laughter! Each costume's labeled, Nate's, 'Sponge Bob', Michael's, Merlin the magician, complete with make-up, wig and mustache and Doe's, Dora the Explorer. Her costume's full body with head piece! Her identity's completely concealed. It's perfect for her! *Since the age of seven she's worn a unique facial mask whenever in public. She was uncomfortable with people gawking at her! As a consequence her public appearance anywhere was rare!* Grant had covered all the bases and their excitement's child-like!

The event's a huge success! The mascots and face painters are a big hit and Michael's magic show is the highlight! Minutes after 7 p.m. the clean up's over, but Grant, Michael and Nate are still conversing with members of the charity and its participants. On the other hand, she just wants to go home, take off the costume, refresh and relax. She eases out of the room and is momentarily lost for direction. After several twists and turns she passes thru double-doors into the erratic activity of the emergency department its sounds of pain, suffering and scents of alcohol and antiseptics. She moves thru cautiously scanning for the exit doors to the parking area and spots them. As she nears they're forced open by an incoming gurney bearing the bloody, battered body of a woman! Doe plasters herself against the door as the EMT holding an IV bag in the air and a hooded doctor on its opposite side rush by! She can hear the doctor offering warm, consoling words of hope and comfort to the victim while calmly dictating life-saving instructions to medical personnel! Whoever she is, she's amazing! The woman's head's heavily bandaged. Due to the tracheotomy rolled up towels versus a standard brace have been carefully placed snugly on each side of her neck for stabilization. Her face's badly swollen and the sheets that cover her are stained with her blood. She's a victim of spousal abuse! Doe watches intently as the gurney's pushed into the nearest vacant triage area followed by doctors, nurses and crash carts! Distracted by the activity she'd neither noticed nor heard the orderly hollering and waving his arm trying to gain her attention! Now she notices. "Hey! Dora Explorer! Will you allow the door to close?" Startled she jumps rushes thru the door, hurries to the parking lot, takes off the headpiece and climbs into the vehicle. Twenty minutes later the guys arrive. As they ride along Grant addresses, "I'm so grateful for your help! Thank-you!" His brow furrows and eyes narrow with faux suspicion, "Am I to be sure none of you are 'moonlighting'? Your performances were more than noteworthy! They felt professional!" They look to each other then back to him and laugh hysterically! "When would we have time? It was our pleasure! Really! It was exactly what we needed." *Unbeknownst to the trio they'd been set-up! Grant had paid the three 'no-shows' for their absence. He wanted to keep them close as long as possible!* The driver activates the gate, turns off of the highway, drives thru and the gate closes behind them. "Anyone up for a nightcap?" Michael offers. "I've got to pass! All I want right now's to get out of this (*she gestures to the suit*) and take a bath!" *Everyone chuckles! They've hardly ever seen her so uncomfortable!* "I have to decline too!" states Grant. Michael looks to Nate, "Well?" Nate gives a quick wink, "I'm in! But just one!" The vehicle pulls to the curb and they climb out. Doe and Grant bid Michael and Nate good-night! She begins stripping as soon as she enters the sanctuary of her suite and moves to the bathroom. She's extremely irritable from the grit and excessive moisture on her skin caused by the suit! Hurriedly she pushes a button and the 'nahaea' begins filling the bathing vessel. It fills quickly and she slithers in.

Doe emerges refreshed, dries off, dons silk pajamas, footies, melts into her comfy chair and presses a button inset on the panel in its arm. It activates the HAD/4D, eighty inch monitor on the wall directly in front of her. *If visible they'd appear to be huge rectangular panes of glass.* Real-time images burst forth! This isn't network television! These transmissions are via the Corporation's system! *The monitors in the rooms and the others were never intended for humanoid broadcasts.* The images are of *Earth.* Doe's filled with sorrow, watching and feeling the pain of the active assault, by Bahleide and BTs, against *her* absent any remorse! She de-activates the monitor and nestles her head into the pillow.

Doe and Nate have always kept a constant watch since their first day of duty. Inspecting images of her via their monitors daily. Comparing their observations to ensure accurate, balanced assessments necessary for the creation of meticulously detailed reports to forward to Command. Michael's presence had altered routine functions for the day! The Corporation's been recording the changes occurring to her for millions of years. Present accumulated data shows shocking and appalling levels of greenhouse gas build-up, disintegration, degeneration, decay and even the onset of rigor mortis in a couple of areas. It's not enough that they've scarred and sickened her! The Bahleide via the BTs truly seek to destroy her!

As they take their last sips Michael offers, "Another?" "No thanks! I'm going to take a shower. I'll be in my room!" "Okay. Me too! Oh, I'm heading out to see Prince in the morning!" Nate turns, "Alright! Be well!"

Upon entering his room Nate activates the audio. Soft sounds of smooth jazz fills the air. After refreshing he dons the bottoms of a grey silk pajama set Michael had given him as a present from Thailand. He yawns, stretches and activates the monitor to check on *her.* He detests what he sees and wonders how much longer *she'll* hold on! Disgusted he turns it off, lays his head on the pillow and closes his eyes!

Michael doesn't share their duty of responsibility, but he too is concerned for *her* and his view's equally depressing! He de-activates the monitor, interlocks his hands, places them behind his head and lays back. Now he understands why they hadn't slept. They're worried and rightly so! He exhales deeply and closes his eyes.

May 3rd

6:04 a.m.

Michael climbs out of bed and activates his audio. The Rascals, 'It's a Beautiful Morning' begins playing as he heads to the bathroom.

After drying off, moisturizing, fragrance and deodorizing he dons a blue and white checkered flannel shirt, blue jeans, soft brown leather vest and shiny, camel cowboy boots. Then opens the door of a specially designed compartment of his armoire and retrieves his favorite Stetson. Lastly, he puts on a peanut butter, ribbed corduroy sports jacket. It's a bit chilly outside! Now he's ready to see Prince, but he must stop by the kitchen en route!

He opens the door of the stable and takes a few steps. Prince rises to his feet and sticks his head over the gate! He recognizes Michael's footfalls and detects his scent! *Shaka and Zephyr are sound asleep.* "Welcome home! Michael, you look great!" he greets excitedly! Michael opens the gate, steps to him and places his arms affectionately about his neck, "Thanks Prince! It's good to be home! I've missed you!" "Nah, dog! I missed you more!" Michael retracts his arms as if stuck by a pin! "Aw man! Juan's been teaching you slang!" He complains as he takes a seat on the plush cot affixed to the back wall of his stall. *Prince laughs!* "Really, Prince! Have you been okay? I have to ask **you**! Because they'd never tell me unless it was a life or death matter and even then they'd be reserved!" *Prince chuckles for a moment!* "I know!" *His voice turns solemn.* "Michael! You're family! They'll always be protective and supportive of you and all things of YOU! But really I've been good! Juan's great! He takes good care of me! I don't know what I'd do without him! *He snorts!* Hey! Uhh…aren't you forgetting something?" He chuckles, reaches into his pockets and pulls out three big red apples. He places them on the hay covered floor before him! "How's your search?"

Prince inquires between chomps. "Slow, but I do have data on several for review!" "Well! That's better than nothing at all! Right?" "Yeah! I guess! Have you talked to Juan yet?" "No! He and I are close, but not t-h-a-t close! I do the horse thing with everyone, except Nate and Doe!" *Michael chuckles!* Prince's ears turn upward and he warns, "Sssh! Someone's coming!" Juan enters the stable. "Welcome home, sir! So good to see you! What'd ya think? Am I taking good care of him?" he questions as he moves to Prince's stall extending his hand. Michael accepts his hand, "Oh yes! Thanks! You're doing an excellent job! He's quite happy with you and he looks marvelous!" *Prince shakes his head and snorts!*

Doe walks down the corridor and knocks on Michael's door. There's no answer. She tries the knob. It opens to a vacant room. She then goes to Nate's suite, knocks and walks in. He's dressed for riding and looking into the mirror adjusting his Stetson. "Nate? Where's Michael?" he turns to her. "He's with the only being that holds more sway with him than you or I!" *She exhales.* "Prince!" "Yup! I'm on my way to join them. You know? It's been sometime since all of us including Shaka and Zephyr have run together!" "Hmm! You're right! I'll change."

This time when she'd returned from the 'Greenwood' she'd brought the horses back too! It was an uncommon action! Normally they'd have remained at Stone Valley for at least four to six months. But for reasons unknown, even to her, she'd been compelled to keep them close!

A few feet away from a wide stream they dismount. Prince, Shaka and Zephyr make their way to the water while the trio seat themselves under a cluster of shading trees and absorb *her* sights and sounds. It's early-morning, the sun's only half awake and there's a gentle breeze. Michael fidgets a bit and exhales, "Really! How's *she?*" Doe's eyes are fixed on the running waters of the stream, "*She's* not good! I know you might think that with our abilities there'd be a better answer! But our hands are tied! We're restricted by the Prime Directive to interfere. It's distressing being forbidden to aid her! She belongs to us as well as the many Tauri who bear our trait! We desire to protect and save every one of them from the Bahleide and BTs." After satisfying their thirst the horses return to them. "Looks like it's time to go!" chuckles Michael as he looks to Doe, Nate then back to the horses! They mount up and ride along each of their favorite trails, race and play tag. It's been some time since they were all together and shared joy, laughter, love and peace! It's the best time they've all had in a long while! As the sun takes her place in the noon sky they decide to return to the stables.

Upon return the stalls have been refreshed and Juan's there to assist Doe with her saddle. "Hey? Don't we deserve assistance too?" Michael taunts. *Juan laughs!* "You guys are too much!" It's after the lunch hour when the horses are settled and they begin walking back. "We've left-overs from last night. Care to join me!" Nate offers. "Sounds like a plan to me!" Doe replies. "Me too!" says Michael.

They've eaten and are sitting about when Michael announces, "I have something for you." Doe looks to Nate puzzled! He looks to her then back to Michael in silence! Michael hands each a folder containing brief background data of four individuals. "What's this?" she questions. He smiles briefly and leaves the room. *For reasons of security there're no photos included.*

CONDENSED DOSSIER OVERVIEWS

Chikoya Oka- Neural Surgeon

Post baccalaureate certificate-John Hopkins University

Doctor of Medicine- George Mason University

Post Master certificate- Weill Cornell Medical

Born- July 7, 1938

Place of birth- Oklahoma Reservation

Eyes-Champagne

*Comments- world renown for not only his skill but his charity.

He responds to the poorest in need of his skill first regardless of their ability to pay.

Hakeem Bryce- Civil Engineer/Architect

Master of Civil Engineering- Norwich University

Master of Science in Electrical and Computer- Stanford University

Master Engineering and Construction- Purdue University

Born- July 7, 1938

Place of birth- Camden, New Jersey

Eyes- Champagne

*Comments- successful civil engineer, architect and consultant. CEO of the 'Ankh', his engineering firm. His designs are flawless and the methods he implements are mystifying. To the firm's credits are two bridges, three convention centers, four hotels and a library. He and his business partner Jonathan Lucien are the creators and sponsors of design workshops for troubled and under-privileged young men/feminine. To their credit all of their participants successfully graduate high school and attend college.

Claire Tamarumaro- Bio-chemist

Chemical Science's Master-University of Pennsylvania

S.B. degree in chemistry-Columbia University

ACS certification in Bio-chemistry

Philosophy and Science Ph.D. -Tufts University

Born- July 7, 1938

Place of birth- Muko, Japan

Eyes- Champagne

*Comments- She's an eminent bio-chemist consultant, martial arts expert and has a network of dojos nation-wide and in France. She's the

founder of 'Victus Academies La Femme', private schools for girls ages seven thru eighteen. Currently there're eight nationwide and three foreign.

Janet Xuan Shang-Brooks, Esquire

Master of Law, L.L.M. - Harvard University

Juris Doctor, J.D. - Oxford University, England

Doctor of Juridical Sciences- George Mason

Born- July 7, 1938

Place of birth- Shang-Da region, China

Eyes- Champagne

*Comments- She's considered the Jonnie Kockron of the courtroom and the founder of a world class, eight-star, catering business which has international branches. She's also the anonymous founder of 'Earth Haven', an outreach network.

After review they look to each other. Their hearts and thoughts race! They're clearly shaken when he returns into the room!

Nate looks to him, "Your work's always been exemplary! But this! Thank-you, Michael! Because of you we may be going home sooner than we'd dare dream!" She questions, "When're they arriving? And which of them do you feel is the *one*?" "They'll be here on Thursday. O-o-o-h! I'm not sure which of them it is!" Michael grimaces slightly, "Did either of you take notice of their eye color and year of birth?" Baffled they scan the information once more and he leaves the room in search of Grant. In their excitement they'd over-looked the key verifying factors! They look to each other with smiles of enormous joy! *This is real! The search is over! Michael had found not one, but all!* "Doe, I'm so excited! I feel like a kid finally getting the chance to play with others like me! Like us! It really doesn't matter if they're elderly! The high point's that they'll understand us and we'll understand them! We'll be able to share ideas and information! We'll be able to commune together! I'm more than anxious to interact with them!"

She smiles! This had been their greatest desire. Yet its reality's surreal after the passage of so much time! They're in varying degrees of shock! Even for them it's much to process that they'll be returning home in less than four years versus twenty with the highest of honors....all of the seedlings! "Alright! Nate, according to the data they're elderly. We've elevators, but we'll need to have walkers, wheelchairs and attendants on standby. Also the menu should be structured for them. Foods easily managed! Can you think of anything else we need to plan for to ensure their comfort?" "No, but I'm certain that between Grant and Michael every consideration for their comfort and safety will be arranged. I still can't believe we're meeting them on Thursday!" "Me either, Nate! But we must be cautious and patient with them." *He rises abruptly!* "Excuse me! But this is so overwhelming! I need solitude right now!" "I understand completely. Me too." They retire to their suites to calm their thoughts that're bouncing around in their minds like ping-pongs at lightning speed!

Michael finds Grant in his office and brings him up to speed. "Uh... Grant when we're done I need to leave immediately! I've got a few matters to tend to!" "Of course, I'll arrange your transport! But aren't you going to bid them farewell?" "No! There's no time!" He also requests that Petra, Jamie and Maxx travel to Locus Angeli to give Mano's crew a rest. Grant orders a craft readied for his departure. *He still has much to do!*

Doe nor Nate could explain the wonderful warm feelings and vibrations they're experiencing! It hadn't existed until the moment they'd taken that second look at the files! This isn't a dress rehearsal and the 'network' *senses* it too!

CHAPTER SEVEN
the invitation

MAY 1ST
6:30 p.m. (time zone specific)

Each *seedling's* visited by a well-groomed, handsome, immaculately dressed, white gloved, male/feminine, courier clutching a finely crafted leather fleece bearing the insignia of the 'Greenwood Corporation'. The courier's greet each by name and informs they've been sent at the request of Michael Fenfox and presents the fleece. Each is acquainted with Michael thru varying circumstances and trust him. They accept the fleece and offer each a tip! The tips are respectfully declined.

Jae's first to receive the invitation. After shutting the door she slouches into her comfy chair and opens the fleece. Inside's a letter and an unsealed 5x7 tan vellum envelope. Inside of it's a matching card with a quarter inch border of embossed feathers highlighted with gold flecks. The feathered borders encased a daytime photo of the corporate beachfront property, 'Locus Angeli', on the island of Caicos.

At the forefront of the photo, sparkling, turquoise waves roll onto a sandy beach. The images are so sharp and colors so vivid it impels her to touch it with the finger of her free hand. On contact she feels the warmth of the water! As she looks closer the waves are actually heaving back and forth and the fronds of the palm trees move gently from an invisible breeze! Startled she quickly withdraws her finger! The motion of the waves and fronds stops! She looks at her fingertip and it's wet! Stunned she stares at the card for a moment before placing it on the end table beside her. She relaxes and tries to make sense of what she's just experienced and falls asleep.

An hour or so later she awakes and instinctively looks to the end table. *'Had she imagined or dreamt the invitation?'* No! Not only is it there! But the photo now reflects sunset! *'This is very advanced technology!' she thinks to herself.* The letter contains detailed instructions and requests their utmost discretion. She gets up, pours a glass of ginger beer, returns to the chair and picks up the phone to R.S.V.P.

The other candidates share similar experiences! They also accept without reservation!

CHAPTER EIGHT

arrival, indoctrination and seduction

MAY 8TH DAY ONE

6:45 a.m.

Plain clothes 'AP' security commandeer local cabs. They collect each from their residence and deliver them to the nearest private airstrip. Due to deliberate scheduling they'll arrive at varying times.

Locus Angeli, Caicos Island

12:15 p.m.

Mano's standing on the verandah fidgeting with his tie as the vehicle carrying the first pulls to the curb. *'It's been years since the last candidates had arrived for review. They'd been good natured, intelligent, compassionate individuals just not who they sought! Is this another dress rehearsal?' he ponders.* Shane opens the rear door and a handsome, male passenger with an East coast (New York/Philadelphia) accentuated tenor voice steps out. "Good-afternoon! I'm Hakeem Bryce!" "Good-afternoon, sir! I'm Shane! Welcome! Welcome! We've been expecting you! Please!" he greets gesturing him to the staircase. He's meticulously attired in a light brown linen/silk blended Vershon designer suit, vanilla silk tee shirt and molasses brown 'old man' comforts that shine like new copper pennies! *Shane glances to the verandah shaking his head and chuckling! Michael had saved the best surprise for last! He'd not mentioned anything in reference to their physical condition. It was quite an unfounded assumption by Doe and Nate that they were elderly though! After all, they still appear much younger (late thirties/early forties) than their centuries!* Mano glances over his shoulder to the staff members standing by and gives them a negative nod. They remove themselves and apparatus! "Welcome! I'm Mano." he greets extending his hand. "Hi! I'm Hakeem Bryce!" *As they clasp hands Mano experiences an extreme sensation for a second! It's Hakeem's LES! It's strong!* "Allow me to show you to your suite. Your hosts will welcome you at the reception. It's at six and dress is casual elegant." After climbing more steps and making a few turns they arrive to the double doors of his suite. Mano hands him the key-card and informs, "Your hosts are aware of your passion for physical fitness and have scheduled a work-out for you! Phil's the name of your trainer. He'll arrive for you in about thirty minutes. Any information you require is available at your media station. *He points to it.* See you this evening!" Mano leaves his presence. Hakeem swipes the card, enters and stands in awe! The outer walls of the room are crystal clear, bullet-proof glass, floor to ceiling drapery runs their length for shading and privacy and the view's breath-taking!

The second arrives as Mano returns to the verandah. Shane opens the rear door. He's speechless at the exotic vision before him! He nearly loses his balance! She's wearing a cream/tawny Mondavi suit and special order four inch Stew Weisser heels. Her coiffure's quite stylish! "Hi! I'm Claire!" she announces in a soft, cheerful Asian accentuated voice. Snapping back to the moment he begs, "Uh…please excuse me! Welcome! I'm Shane." He offers his arm, escorts and introduces her to Mano. "Welcome Claire! We've been expecting you! Allow me to show you to your suite! Madam's scheduled a special 'spa' session for you! Nick will arrive for you…etc." *He experiences a sensation from her too, but it's nothing like that of Hakeem!*

There's no vehicle when he returns to the verandah. Within seconds it curves around the bend. Shane opens the door and can only stare as he assists her! "How kind of you! Thank-you! I'm Janet!" she offers with a soft smile and an inflection he's unable to pinpoint! She's wearing a

Mondavi original white linen suit and plum designer heels by Memphisto II. She's beyond seductive! He quickly recovers and escorts her to Mano who's wiping his brow as they near. He's sweating profusely and it's not the weather! But the heat of this one's spirit! Shane introduces, "Mano! This is Miss Janet Xuan Shang-Brooks." Mano smiles broadly and his eyes twinkle, "Welcome! Welcome Miss Shang-Brooks! We've been expecting you!" "Oh, please! Call me Jae. I insist!" "Very well, Jae! Allow me to show you to your suite!" He offers his arm and recants what he's shared with Claire as they walk along and alerts her to the spa appointment. "I look forward to seeing you this evening!" *He reaches for his handkerchief as he walks away.*

Chikoya's already out of the vehicle when he returns. He's immaculately attired in an Armondo cream silk suit, chocolate shirt, two-tone necktie and mocha slip-ons! He's entrancing! *Both Mano and Shane feel his LES! The hairs of their skin stand on end and they look to each other! Who is this?* "Hi! I'm Chikoya Oka. My friend's call me 'Ko'!" he informs with an outstretched hand and a smile! Shane grasps his hand, "Welcome! We've been expecting you! I'm Shane. Please!" he implores gesturing to the staircase. He climbs and is met by Mano's outstretched hand, "Welcome, Dr. Oka! I'm Mano. Please allow me to show you to your suite!" "I'm at your command! And please! Call me 'Ko.'"

Mano Kabali's an imposing man of Filipino and Norwegian heritage. He's in charge at 'Locus Angeli' with the authority equal to Grant's at 'Angel Place'. Cathy Beal had recruited him and he'd recruited Shane Murdock, as the head of security. Shane's a native of Samoa. Both men are immaculately attired, six-breasted, cream white, light-weight linen suits, matching vests and white silk tee-shirts accented by bone suede footwear! *Neither Mano nor Shane alert the Beals regarding the condition of their guests or Michael's arrival!*

5:45 p.m.

Michael and Mano are standing in the reception area discussing operations scheduling when Hakeem descends. "Hello, Hakeem! It's good to see you again! It's been a while!" Michael greets. *At that moment Hakeem can't place him in his memory. He's clearly baffled!* "Come on now! *He goads.* We met at-" *Finally it kicks in and he blurts.* "I...I remember now! Brad Chriton introduced us at the (AAW) Americas Architect Awards. *(That'd been nearly a year ago!)* I complimented you on the suit you were wearing and mentioned I'd like to have one!" "Yes, that's right! I have it with me!" *His jaw drops!* Michael looks pass him to the staircase. A voice inside his head bellows, *wow!* As she clears the last step he gently grasps her hands and kisses her cheeks, "Hi Jae! You look amazing!" She locks eyes with him and smiles, "I had a feeling you were behind this! Oh! I'd like to discuss that invitation later, too! Mmm...what're you wearing? It's intoxicating!" *He chuckles!* "Girl! You better stop playing with me!" *Mano clears his throat! Michael understands his meaning.* "Oh! Forgive my manners. Janet, this is Hakeem Bryce." *Hakeem blindly offers his hand, his eyes are all over her!* "The pleasure's all mine! I assure you!" "It's nice to meet you! And please, call me 'Jae!" Claire's midway of her descent when she hears Jae's voice and pauses for a moment! Then chalks it up to her imagination and continues. Michael cuts his eyes to Claire as she clears the last step. "Jae! Here's someone I...think you know!" *She turns.* Both gasp and give Michael the *look!* "You're just chock full of surprises aren't you?" Claire quips. As they embrace he whispers, "Mmmm! G-i-r-l you look yummy!" She shakes her head and chuckles as they release, "You're still bad!" Smiling Michael looks to Hakeem and introduces, "This is Claire!" Hakeem gently takes her hand, "It's my pleasure!" He then looks to Michael in astonishment! "Man! Where? How do you find such lovely ladies?" An odd sensation rips thru the group like an electric current causing goose bumps and hairs to stand on end! They look one to another! It's Chikoya descending!

Jae's dumbfounded! Claire's in shock! Hakeem's smiles! Michael and Mano glance to each other with smiles of knowing! No sooner than he clears the last step he moves to Jae. "Hi! It's a wonderful surprise to see you! How's Ivory?" She smiles briefly, "It's good to see you too and Ivory's fine! The last time we saw you was on the news!" Claire interrupts, "The rest of us would like to meet him, Jae!" "Oh! Sorry! Claire, this is Dr. Chikoya Oka!" *He smiles to her!* "It's a pleasure to meet you Claire and please call me Ko!" While Hakeem and Ko exchange handshakes and man-hugs Jae moves to Claire's side, "That's Ivory's hunk! The guy I was telling you about from her flight!" Claire looks to her faking envy! "Girl! It ain't right! It just ain't fair! How does she do it?" They shake their heads in joint resignation! *Each had honored the request for discretion regarding their invitation and are beyond surprised and happy to see each other!* "Okay! Let's go! There're others anxious to meet you!" Mano informs. They travel down the corridor and arrive to the grand reception room. As they're entering Claire looks about. "Mano? Are you expecting dignitaries?" With a broad smile he replies, "Oh, no Claire! These honorees are heavier hitters than dignitaries! This is in honor of you! All of you!" They're paralyzed with shock! The room's filled with a rainbow of no less than two hundred or so feminine and males, uniformed security and plain clothed residential and non-residential personnel anxious to meet them.

6:39 p.m.

She's sitting in her room despondent when he enters. "I waited at the landing. When you didn't arrive I checked the 'Morning' room. You weren't there so I kinda thought I might find you here!" He seats himself beside her and takes her hand. "Is this what you call casual elegant? Really? You look fantastic! Got a hot date?" She glances to him void of laughter. "Maybe you should go without me." she suggests sullen. "What is it? What's wrong?" *She exhales.* "That's the problem! Nate! I've no idea! I don't know! I just feel very strange!" *He sighs.* "Well! We've four guests waiting for their hosts and we're late! It wouldn't be right not to welcome them!" Reluctantly she concedes.

As they approach the staircase she pauses and turns to him, "I thought Michael would be here?" He smiles to her, "He's here! He wanted to surprise you!" "He's got to stop this! I can't take too many more of his surprises!" Nate nods, "Ain't that the truth!" The music's somewhat audible as they near the reception and it's not the classical works of Florence Price! They look to each other baffled! *They'd considered everything and decided classical would be most appropriate. But what they're hearing's party music!* "What's going on?" she challenges. "That's a good question!" Michael's coming out of the reception room as they're about to enter and freezes momentarily, "Whoa! Wow! You guys look g-o-o-d! I was just coming to find you! Come on!" he urges entwining her arm with his own. They observe a lavishly decorated, elegantly set semi-circle banquet table front center encircled by eight others. The dance floor at the rear's crowded with bodies swirling, gyrating to the music! *They see no elderly!* Nate looks to Michael "Where're our guests?" he challenges curtly. Michael points to the dance floor, "They're out there! Except Janet!" he replies pointing to where she sits. As they look to her Doe wavers slightly like a twig touched by a strong but gentle breeze! Nate notices, grasps her gently and steadies her! "Are you okay?" She glances to him, "I'm fine! Why do you ask?" *In that moment he realizes she's no recollection of what's just occurred!* "Come!" Michael invites leading the way. *He'd not seen her waver!*

Jae's busy watching everyone dance, grooving to the music and doesn't notice them nearing. Michael calls out to her! She turns with a smile and a strange, wonderful sensation washes over her causing a mild jerking motion within her for a fleeting moment, then her eyes fall upon the Beals! They're immaculately attired and stunningly handsome each in their own right and they've a glow! Nate and Michael get a sudden case of 'ants in the pants' as the music changes! "Will you ladies please excuse us?" They don't wait for their answers! Doe looks to Jae, "Seems we've been abandoned! Hello! I'm Dora! I prefer to be called Doe. May I sit?" she inquires in a sultry, French accentuated voice. "Oh, I'm so sorry! Please! Forgive my manners! I'm Janet, but I prefer Jae!" Doe looks to her with an easy smile!

TRAIT

"Hmp! What they just did to us is nothing I assure you! How was your travel?" "Madam! First I want to thank-you ever so much for your generous invitation! It was more than kind of you to arrange the spa treatment! I didn't realize just how tense and exhausted I was until Ming (*the masseuse*) worked my kinks out!" "Oh, my dear! It was our pleasure! I'm glad it was to your liking! Ming is the best though! Agreed?" "Agreed!" "And Jae! Please! Never again address me as madam. You make me sound old!" Jae nods with a smile!

Nate returns to the table with Hakeem in tow, "Doe, this is Hakeem Bryce. Hakeem, this is your host and my sister, Dora!" She offers her hand. Instead of shaking it he gently grasps it and cradles it in his own. Then bends slightly and presses it to his lips! She's taken aback! "Oh my goodness! Another smooth operator!" she comments with a moderate shake of her head. His eyes dance as he smiles to her! "Madam! Thank-you for your generous invitation! For me this is beyond therapeutic!" *Nate's fixated on him. He's already in love with his mind! He's questions about the techniques he applies!* She smiles into his eyes, "It's our pleasure! I trust your travel was tolerable and that accommodations are of comfort! Oh! And please call me, Doe!" He smiles, "My lady, everything's fine! Just like you!" *She chuckles.* "Nate! He's definitely 'light-headed'! He must be hungry!" *Laughter erupts!* "Hmmm! Food...the aromas have been teasing my senses since entering the room!" Jae mumbles. *Doe's surprised they've not eaten!* "My goodness! None of you have eaten? You must be starved!" Michael returns to the table clasping Claire's hand. He introduces, "Claire this is your hostess, my sister Dora." *The two women smile one to another.* "It's more than a pleasure to meet you! Thank-you for inviting me, Miss Beal!" "It's our pleasure! And please...call me Doe, okay?" *Claire nods!* He's been standing motionless with his eyes fixated on her! Michael gently elbows him and he rouses, "Chikoya, this is your hostess and my sister, Dora." "Uhh...I'm s-o sorry dear lady! Please forgive! But he didn't warn you were such a lovely creature! It's beyond a pleasure to meet you! And please! I insist you call, me Ko!" he implores as he kisses her hand. "O-o-h, n-o-o! Please call

67

my guards! I'm under threat from not one, but two Don Juan's who'd test my virginal fortitude! Wait! Do you and Hakeem suffer the same illness?" *Laughter again erupts!* Mano finally makes his way to the table where they sit. She shoots a darting glance at him and he throws up his hands in mock surrender! "What? What?" "They haven't had a morsel to eat! Surely, they're hungry! I know I am!" she protests. "My lady! We were waiting on you!" he quips calmly! *He'd landed a home-run with that zinger!* With a bit of attitude she concedes, "Okay! Well! I'm here now!" He turns and hollers to the room, "Chow time!" *She frowns and gives him a hard stare!*

The air was void of hums of conversations while they ate and drank. After sating their hunger the hums begin again as they enjoy desserts! "I really feel like dancing!" Michael announces. He rises, moves to the console and activates it. Then returns to the table and grabs Claire's hand. The music begins as they hit the dance floor! Before long everyone's dancing! All except Doe.

After a few songs Jae leaves Nate, her present dance partner, and goes over to Doe. "Come on!" she urges gently tugging on her hand! "This is a good line song!" All eyes suddenly shift, some even stop dancing awaiting her reaction! They weren't and she wasn't accustomed to anyone touching, much less tugging on her! All alarms are dispelled as she smiles and surrenders! After the dance she excuses herself and disappears from the room for a time.

Minutes after eleven everyone bids good-night and the *candidates* return to their suites. Their beds have been turned down and a white powdered, ginger jellied candy lay atop their pillows.

Nate doesn't go straight to his suite, but detours to Doe's. He knocks softly on the door, "It's open!" she offers in a soft voice. "I figured it was you." "Well! What do think?" he challenges taking the seat next to her at the bar. She cocks her head slightly and gives a faux stare of suspicion before growing a smile! "It's them!" He smiles and kisses her forehead. It startles her! "What'd I do to deserve that?" "You came to life tonight!" he comments gleefully as he exits. She smiles realizing something indeed has changed!

May 9th Day Two

She stretches, squints to the clock....9:45 and jumps up to refresh. Parrot's Bay's (*one of three premier cafés*) empty when she arrives at 10:50! Then she recalls Michael organizing last night's '*willing*' to *surf* with him today! She'd declined for obvious reasons, but Claire had been undecided.

Surfing with Michael meant stopping and partying at every establishment from the most humble and traditional, to the most lavish!! Anyone accompanying him is treated and accepted as family and everything's on the house! He knows everyone! Most times it was him plus one. Today, he had a family!

She ponders, '*If Claire had decided to go?*' Malik notices her descending the staircase while walking thru the first floor corridor. *He's resident staff and was in attendance last night.* He smiles to her, "Good-morning, ma'am! You're beautiful as always! Last night was really great! You okay?" "Good-morning, Malik! Oh yes! I'm fine! Everybody gone?" "Yes, sir! Except for Claire! She's either in the cabana or out on the beach!" "Oh! Thank-you!"

Jamie, Petra and Maxx are busy checking inventory when Maxx catches a glimpse of her, from the corner of her eye, nearing them from the rear. She turns and greets, "Well! Good-morning, ma' lady! How ya feelin? It was really a great party last night! And you looked wonderful!" Jamie interrupts excitedly, "Claire, Hakeem, Jae and Ko are very good people! We like them!" "Yes! A blind man could see that!" she retorts with heavy sarcasm. They look to each other shocked by her tone! *Ouch!* Maxx spins around and gives her a hard look, "Uh, o-o-h! Somebody's a bit salty! This isn't like you! One of them is pulling on your heart, huh? Its Hakeem isn't it? I can understand it! He's f-i-n-e, smart and fun! H-m-m-p! H-m-m-p! H-m-m-p!" *Doe looks away.* But Jamie had hit a nerve! "Commander, please! Go

69

to the cabana. I'll bring something to lift your spirits!" Maxx offers consolatory. Doe grimaces, but follows her suggestion.

They prop up against the edges of the counter tops with arms folded and wait! Silent for minutes to ensure she's out of range before speaking in hushed voices. Maxx looks to them, "I never thought we'd see that! But the girl's got the fever!" "Yeah! I think you're right! We've never heard that tone before! Ever! You think we'll still have our jobs when we get back?" Petra queries. Jamie chuckles as she looks to Maxx, "Now do you believe Petra's special?" Maxx chuckles and nods, "Petra calm down. Sure, we'll have them! She's just frightened! She doesn't know how to handle her feelings. This is new to her! Hell! This is new to us! It's kind of cute though! Think about it! After all this time she's never shown any intimate interest in anybody! But she got testy with us because we said we liked them! We never even mentioned anyone in particular!" Petra shakes her head defiantly, "Uh huh, Maxx! You said, Hakeem!" "O-o-h yeah!" Maxx comments reflecting.

"Anyway, she definitely desires one of them! Now the real question's which one? We'll dwell on that mystery later. Right now! We'd better whip up something good and fast! Cause' she's got a short fuse this morning y'all!" They chuckle and set straight to work preparing comfort food!

Claire's reclining in a chaise lounge listening to the soothing sounds of nature when Doe enters the cabana. "Claire, you didn't go *surfing*?" She raises up and casts a quick glance to her. "No. I just wanted to rest. Especially after last night! It was great! I really had a good time!" "Mind if I join you?" "Oh, no! Not at all! Please!" She reclines in the chaise next to her.

Minutes later, Maxx enters with two trays bearing four Mimosas, two sixteen ounce glasses of ice water, pastries and assorted fruits. She places them on two small bamboo tables they share. "Here's a little something to enjoy!" "How sweet and thoughtful! Thank-you!" Claire remarks cheerfully. Maxx eyes Doe, "Call me if you need anything, madam!" Doe glares acknowledgment of her sarcasm! *Maxx can't help snickering as she walks away! She'd actually been pouty!*

They're lulled into full relaxation by the soft, silk covered, over-stuffed cushions of the chaise combined with their drinks plus hors d'oeuvres. Claire probes, "Can I ask you a personal question?" Doe turns to her, "Why of course! You can ask me anything! But first! I must know! Who's your designer? I really adored what you wore last evening!" A bit shocked by her inquiry Claire returns, "Oh! Mondavi!" *Doe's taken aback and it shows on her face!* "No! You've got to be kidding! He's my designer too! I wear him exclusively!" "So do Jae and I!" "I felt a familiarity in your attire! Uh…Claire? What was your question?" "You've answered it! I really loved what you wore last night too!" "Why thank-you! So tell me? How's the attendance and performance at your academies? Any problems?" "You know about me?" *She smiles!* "Yes! I like to know about my friends!" "Well! The students are fine! I have a great staff, but I'd like to be able to provide protection to and from school for them. Give them physical safety and mental comfort! I wish I could offer financial support and employment services to them, their families and to create 'eco-buds'. Eco-buds would be the name I'd assign to groups of students who'd collect trash and debris in their areas over-weekends to beautify them. I'd pay them a modest sum. Lastly, I'd like to teach them ecology and how to plant trees." Doe's been listening intently, but it's her mention of 'trees' that perks her up! "It's odd that you should mention 'trees'! Vaughn Burtron invited me to accompany him on an investigative eco-tour in Bangladesh a few weeks ago. They're experiencing catastrophic devastation resulting from de-forestation! A moratorium should've been placed on them and other natural resources around the world seventy-five years ago! *Both exhale in sorrow for her!* We'll put something together for your schools before you leave!" Claire's shocked! "Thank-you! That's very generous of you! I don't know what to say?" "Nothing need be said. I'm glad we can help!" "Uh…Doe? Were you speaking of the conservationist/ecologist Burtron?" "Yes." "Wow! Tell me! Does Nate share the same interest?" *Are you kidding? He travels routinely* to South Americas to visually inspect the rainforests and collect soil, water and plant samples for analysis. Likewise, he cruises the Amazon." Their conversation's interrupted briefly as Jamie enters with more hors doeuvres; lobster bites, coconut shrimp and steamed, buttered Island mussels and rum drinks.

12:45 p.m.

The surfers have just arrived to their third stop, the 'Coconut Tree'. A traditional hut-type structure of bamboo tucked into the island's easterly mountains, a 'party house'! Its great food, magic drinks, wonderful atmosphere set inside a tropical forest! Ona, one of the owners, offers to guide Jae and Angela on a tour of the falls. They accept and follow her along a winding, spiral path until they reach the fenced clearing at the apex and hear the roar of rushing waters. They look over the fence to a spectacular view! Below lies a pool fed by the cascading waters of the falls bordered by huge boulders! They're in awe! "Come on ladies!" They make their way down the snaking path to the pool and seat themselves on the boulders. Jae glances to Ona then back to the falls, "This is beautiful!" "I thought you'd like it!" Each absorbs the tranquility. "Ona! How're you doing?" Angela probes with sympathy breaking the silence. Ona looks to her saddened, "I come here a lot lately! I think it's responsible for my sanity!" Jae looks to them confused, "What's wrong?" Angela looks to her, "Last weekend two of Ona's employees were murdered because of who they loved!" Jae grimaces shaking her head, "I'm so tired of all the prejudice and injustice. It shouldn't be. I'm very sorry for your lost Ona! Is there anything I can do to help?" "That's very generous of you! But I'll have to check back with you! I'm not certain of their family's needs at this moment! We're all still shell-shocked!" "That's fine! Whenever you need you'll have my number!" Angela looks to each of them, "You know y'all? The world's going to hell on a bloody rollercoaster! Children can't go to school in peace! Every idiot and his brother has an unnecessary gun! And we've gone from a society of compassion to one of greed! Society as a whole suffers from a disease more debilitating and deadlier than Ebola! We've reached critical mass!"

They rest mentally and physically lounge for a long while before Angela checks the time…2:50 p.m. "Whoa! We should head back."

At the cabana…

Sometime after 5 p.m. they're awakened by the coolness of the early evening breeze. Claire yawns with a chuckle, "We feel asleep!" "Aahh…yes! And it was really good!" Doe comments stretching. "I agree completely!" adds Claire looking about. "Seems they're not back yet! I'm going to refresh and settle in for the night. I'm still full as a tick! It's been a wonderful day!" "I share your feelings and I'm going to follow your lead! Honestly! There's no telling how late it'll be when they return! But trust me! They're having a ball! Michael's 'Mr. Party'!" "Oh! I don't doubt it for a minute! That's why I'm saying good-night!" They laugh! "Claire, today was delightful! See you in the morning! Be well!" Claire's bed has not yet been turned down when she arrives to her suite, but there's a glass of water and a jellied candy on the nightstand.

Lo and behold! The Navigators pull up at 9:45 p.m! The 'surfers' empty out happy and loud! The effect of too many umbrella drinks! They're definitely slower, unsteady and beyond loopy! *A jellied candy and a glass of water also awaits them.*

τhe assaulτ

FRIDAY, MAY 9TH
Philadelphia, Pennsylvania
7:40 p.m.

While Hakeem's *surfing* the island with Michael and the others, it's a rainy evening back in' Philly'. His business partner, Jonathan and several of the 'princes' are in the center city office gathering supplies for Saturday's workshop when they're interrupted by the intrusion of six hooded hoodlums! The two at the front of the pack have weapons drawn! Startled Jonathan and the young men submissively throw up their hands in silence and lower their eyes! One of the two thugs at the front looks about and turns to a hooded one at his rear, "What the fuck's this? Bitch! This ain't no fucking bar and grill! Motherfucker!" The thug beside the foul-mouthed one's jumpy and his nervous finger touches the hairpin trigger causing several rounds to expel! Jonathan and the princes duck, but not fast enough! Blood spurts everywhere! One bullet grazes Prince Dokie in the arm and two hit Jonathan! One lodges in his shoulder, the other in his head! It's their blood that lands on the others and continues to flow lava-like! The uninjured princes take off their shirts, undershirts and begin tearing them into strips for bandages and tourniquets as they rapidly apply first aid! They manage to prop Jonathan up in an effort to slow his bleeding. *They'd learned first aid as a part of enrichment during the week-end workshops.*

The princes are attending to their friends and don't see the hoodlums, positioned in behind the itchy-fingered and foul mouthed thugs, pull out small devices *not guns* and point at them. *There's no flash! No sound!*

Without warning the thugs crash to the floor face first and howl in agony! Reflexively their hands opened causing the weapons to catapult thru the air and land on the floor out of reach! At that very moment, three figures, dressed in grey, appear at the rear of the pack! They pull out different devices, point and exit. The devices paralyzed the four in the blink of an eye! They cannot move and though their mouths are agape their screams are mute! Their clothing sags as their bodies begin decomposing!

When the princes do look up for more trouble the two thugs remain helpless on the floor. There's no sign of the others, but an odd stench dominates the room! *The distant screams of sirens grows louder! Who'd called? Hakeem and Jonathan address the young men under their tutelage as 'princes' and the few feminine as 'princesses'! It's their way of reinforcing and instilling dignity and pride!*

7:59 p.m.

Philadelphia's finest come to a screeching halt in front of 4000 Chestnut Street lights flashing! They race out of their vehicles, releasing the restraints and drawing their weapons as they enter the building. They notice treaded boot patterns created by wet soles. There're two distinct sets. No more! The crime team takes pictures and dust for fingerprints. They follow the moans of pain they hear and begin to smell an odor that causes some to place their hands across their faces, reach for handkerchiefs or vomit into trash cans! After a few more steps they see Jonathan and 'Prince Dokie' propped up in a corner surrounded by the others. The injured hoods have soiled their trousers and squirm on the floor unable to move! Four small piles of a pinkish-brown substance lay about the room and are the source of the stench! A haz-mat team had also been requested! But by who?

Despite the rain there're witnesses. They recount seeing six persons get out of a silver late model Escalade, wearing black hoodies and gloves, enter the building as they passed by en route to their individual destinations, but could not see their faces. The F.I.B. and N.I.A. are contacted immediately!

Three weeks earlier the same vehicle had been identified in connection with the fatal hit and run of a senator's son. All state and federal agencies have been on a relentless hunt for the vehicle, its driver and occupants since!

The injured are loaded into ambulances. The uninjured are given blankets and loaded into patrol cars that follow to the nearest hospital. The police department's tow truck arrives and impounds the abandoned vehicle!

Agents Dave Grayson and Robert Deevers of the F.I.B. are presently in the Philadelphia office at 3408 Roosevelt Boulevard on another matter when the call comes in pertaining to the 'nationally hunted' vehicle! "We're on it!" Deevers tells Brad Newsome, the agent beside him, as he snatches his key fob and jacket. Likewise, Grayson grabs his coat and they dash thru the office to the parking lot!

There're still officers present at the scene when they arrive. They direct them to the hospital where the incident officers and detectives await the permission of the attending physician to interrogate the victims and the scum. Grayson and Deevers race back to the car and speed off! They've questions too!

They arrive to the emergency room and introduce themselves to Philadelphia Detectives Richie Johnson and Bob O'Mallee. Det. Johnson shares the information they've so far, which isn't much! The uninjured princes didn't provide much information! They'd been focused on caring for their friends. *But they'd seen something!* The injured hoods have been identified as Dickey Smith aka Gott and Pete Wood aka Twiddles. Both are light-weight offenders! Murder was not nor had it ever been their M.O.!

8:43 p.m.

The 'princes' are in a moderate state of shock. A well-dressed man reeking authority enters the lobby of the hospital and moves to the reception desk. He's Marchall Thergoode, one of the most prominent lawyers on the East coast and an example of a 'light' Tauri. He identifies himself as their legal counsel and demands their whereabouts. With little delay he's led to a small room where they sit shaken! He addresses each by title and name with uncommon familiarity, "Prince Maurice, William, Joseph and Ahmed, Hakeem wants you to know he's sorry about all of this!" Ahmed grimaces and rants, "Sir's sorry? For what? He's not to blame for this!" "I know! But in his world, nothing's ever to touch those he holds dear!" he remarks calmly. He looks about for reasons of privacy and questions in a low voice, "Do you remember anything that you didn't tell the police?" Sheepishly they look to each other and nod! "Sir, the strangers that did whatever to the four goons were women dressed in gray! Not men! But the two paralyzed thugs were injured by the goons they'd came with. And sir! The goons weren't men! It was scary! We don't know what they were!" whispers Prince Maurice. Marchall nods, "We'll keep that between us for now! I'm going to check with the officers and see if they need to speak further with any of you! If not I'm taking you guys home!" They're shocked that he's not surprised by their answers and stoic at the same time. He notices their mood and probes, "What's wrong?" "Well, sir! We've not heard any news concerning Mr. Jonathan's condition!" states Ahmed clearly agitated and gravely concerned! He gives them a calming glance, "Oh! No worries! He's going to be just fine!" *For the first time since the chaos began they exhale deeply and relax!* Prince Maurice frowns, "Sir! You weren't shaken by our account of the others!" He looks to each, "Speak none of this to any other! Hakeem will explain." They nod understanding. *They're Tauri.*

Since the officers have no further questions or reason to detain them they're released and he escorts them to his limousine. They're shocked when he orders them to load in and allows them to experiment with some of its *special features*! It's the first time any of them have ridden in a limousine much less one such as this! He takes them thru the drive-ins of their favorite fast food places and allows them to use the vehicle's phone to order pick-ups! They absorb every moment of the ride. They don't lean out of its windows nor its rooftop, but absorb what they see! After picking up their orders he delivers each to their door, explains to their parents/guardians what's occurred and assures their safety! Like the gentlemen they've been groomed to be each thanks him and shakes his hand. He fights back tears of joy and pride at the results of Hakeem and Jonathan's efforts! If these young men were a reflection of the future, with little doubt everything was going to be just fine!

9:37 p.m.

Dr. Gialotti updates the agents and detectives on the conditions of the perpetrators and grants clearance to interrogate them. He reports that Dokie's injury albeit serious he'd suffered no permanent arterial damage and they can speak with him within the hour. The bullet's been removed from Jonathan's shoulder, but he's in critical condition due to the location of the bullet that's lodged in his head. They'll have to wait! He's induced into a coma to stall for time! He requires the services of a skilled neural surgeon to remove it if he's to live! Gialotti further informs that the x-rays of the thugs revealed precision, razor-like severances of their spinal cords! Yet! There's no scar tissue or evidence of prior surgery! They appear natural! None of the medical personnel has ever seen anything like this! The thugs are placed in separate rooms without cuffs. They weren't going anywhere! They crowd into each room to hear and record their statements. Both recount the same story:

'They were sitting on the corner when the Escalade pulled up to the curb. The stranger on the passenger side rolled down the window and beckoned them. He showed them a wad of hundred dollar bills and said they could earn one for a few hours of work! He claimed they were going to rob the safe of a drug dealer who was out of town! He said that two of their crew had been arrested earlier that day which was why they were recruiting us! Since they didn't have jobs or high school diplomas they accepted the offer. Hustling was the only thing they knew! They've no idea what happened to the strangers and only remember the searing sensation and unbearable pressure on their backs, falling face first to the floor, then being unable to move.'

The agents and detectives look to each other speechless! Det. Johnson assures they'll perform a complete investigation and suggest they meet within a week. Deevers and Grayson agree, but insist on taking the vehicle and the unidentified substance for analysis by their forensic lab. All's agreed upon and they depart Philadelphia that evening to return to their home office in Harrisburg, Pennsylvania. They'll submit their report to the director, David Morrison, first thing Monday morning.

CHAPTER TEN
ınὸoctrınatıon
anὸ seὸuctıon

DAY THREE MAY 10TH
continued
5:05 a.m.

She rises and prepares for the day. Once she's completed grooming she calls Jonas. They've much to discuss and arrange before the *surfers* awake!

A little after ten satisfied with future plans and present progress their communication ends. She heads to the 'Mango Room' (*another café*). Claire, Ko, Hakeem and Michael are seated at a table when she enters applauding mockingly! "Congrats! You survived the '*surf*'!" *Michael eye rolls!* The others lower their heads and snicker! "Yes! We managed thank-you!" retorts the laughing voice in back of her. It's Jae! "Good-morning, Doe!" she greets with a tinge of sarcasm as she passes by her to join the others. *Doe shoots a darting glance to her!* Hakeem detects tension and looks about, "Hey? Where's Nate?" "Well, Jae! Where is he?" Doe challenges. "Yeah! That's a good question!" chimes Claire. Michael and Hakeem look to Ko. *They feel a cat fight brewing!* He runs interference, "Uh…Doe? Just how many relatives does Michael have? Everyone claims him as their own!" Distracted she chuckles, "Ohh! He's a charmer!" Their laughter and chatter ceases as Nate enters. His expression's guarded to say the least as he beckons him. "Ah…excuse me!" Ko begs of the group as he follows him out into the corridor. *Their invitations had requested they leave their personal devices behind, but they were given emergency contact numbers to pass on to their business partners or close associates.*

Nate informs him that Nikki'd called late last night and several times earlier this morning in an effort to reach him. The Sally Henson Medical Center (their employer) had contacted her hoping she could contact him because the mayor of Philadelphia, Pennsylvania knows of his surgical gift and is requesting his services at any cost! The patient's one of the mayor's prominent constituent's! He's the victim of a life threatening head injury resulting from a senseless act of violence. "I took the liberty of calling her. She's seen the scans and other imagery and says you probably are the only one who can attempt to remove it successfully. The man's forty years old and has no existing health problems." He looks him directly in the eyes and pauses, "Now comes the difficult truth! It's Jonathan. Jonathan Lucien." At the mention of 'Lucien' his legs buckle! Nate grabs and steadies him. He grimaces! "Say no more! I'm going." "I know! Transportation will be here in twenty and the airstrip's preparing for your departure! No need to pack, follow me!" They go to Nate's room. Once inside he moves to a small stainless steel-like rectangle on the wall and presses it. A small drawer protrudes and he reaches inside it. He withdraws two small vials, one filled with a brown and the other filled with a violet substance and an empty ampoule. He hands the brown one to him, "Please drink this!" Without question Ko uncaps it and drinks. "You just sampled my creation. I call it 'Pushae'. It's something on the order of a vitamin supplement with *maipen!*"

He'd deliberately left out the fact that it contained 95% Zauton. Nate then uncaps the other via, fills the ampoule with its substance and hands it to him. "This is for Jonathan. Trust me! You'll find its qualities quite helpful. Just add it to the IV." "Ok. Thank-you, Nate! But I need to know just how long it's going to take for me to get there! I've got to call my assistant!" "She's already there. The fastest we can get you there's an hour and a half. Then tack on fifteen minutes to disembark once you land. You'll be traveling via ambulance directly from the plane. So you should be to the hospital within two and a half hours after lift-off. I know how special he's to both of you!" "Wow! You've thought of everything!" "Just trying to help! And don't worry! I'll think of something to tell the group!"

Of course, the group's extremely curious to know what's going on! Especially, Doe! She's totally out of the loop! He's en route to the airstrip as Nate re-enters the 'lion's den'! *He can feel their probing eyes!* He averts eye contact, as much as possible, especially with Hakeem as he informs them of the situation, not the identity of the victim. He reiterates, "Ko said for us to continue as usual and he'll catch up when he returns!" *Hakeem chuckles!* "That's Ko! And he means it!" *Everyone laughs except Doe! She glances to Nate then back to the others.* "How about we meet on the cabana in an hour?" she suggests. All acquiesce and disperse. *Nate exits swiftly and heads for the sanctuary of his suite.* She forces herself to walk out as calmly as possible! She'd much rather fly!

He's on the balcony, looking out across the water in contemplation, when she explodes thru the door to his side, "What's going on?" He looks to her impassive, "Its Jonathan! Jonathan Lucien! He's the patient requiring Ko's surgical skill!" Her body goes limp and falls backward! She lands, just enough, on the edge of an over-stuffed chair to break the fall! *Jonathan's not only Hakeem's business partner, but his longtime friend as is Ko! Together they're brothers of different mothers and know each other very well! They love as brothers!* "We can't tell him! Not yet! Not now!" she protests slightly raising her voice. "Sssh…Calm down! Lower your voice!" He looks into her eyes, "Doe? What've you done? Have you begun the 'therapy'?" She gives him the *look* and challenges, "Of course! Why? What? Was I supposed to wait? For what? Isn't this what we've been hoping and searching for? We're on our way home!" He flops down in the chair next to her and exhales deeply. "You're correct! Forgive my tone! Please!" Her tone softens, "No worries! But to tell him now is an unacceptable, needless risk! A recovered Jonathan will be the one to tell him!" *Nate nods.* "So tell me! How you're administering it?" "Sixty ccs with a mild sedating element given at bedtime. The quicker they enter the state of sleep the faster it acts! It's in the form of a jellied candy." "Very nice! Any negative affects?" "No! They're doing surprisingly well!" "Uh, Doe! I gave Chikoya a huge dose of '*Pushae*' before he left!" *She smiles.* "Well done! So tell me what happened? Are those responsible apprehended?" "Well, yes and no! Eyewitnesses reported seeing at least six hooded persons entering the building. But when the police got there only two of the perpetrators were present. They couldn't escape. Their spinal cords were severed! (*His eyes narrow*)

However, the most disturbing piece of the report are the piles of an unknown, foul smelling substance!" Her eyes flash and a worrying expression appears on her face. *'They're getting closer! Too close! They're still committed to the hunt and their destruction! Only then will they be free to consume the population and destroy Earth! They've been unsuccessful in their efforts to present!'* "Nate! It's time to go sailing. All of us need the safety of the water and peace!" He gives her a concerning *look* and nods agreement.

Ko boards the Cessna, the attendant secures the hatch and the pilot maneuvers into take-off position. He's sound asleep as they lift-off the runway!

CHAPTER ELEVEN
emeRɜency assistance

MAY 10TH

2:35 p.m. entering Philadelphia airspace
Ko's arrival's known only to Dr. Gialotti who's been contacted by Jonas.

He's a tad disoriented as the attendant nudges his shoulder and informs they're on the descent to Philadelphia International. After landing he disembarks and climbs into the ambulance. It peels off, lights flashing, sirens blaring and zips along the Schuylkill expressway unimpeded, traffic pulling to the side when necessary! It exits the center city ramp and speeds to Pennsylvania General's Emergency.

3:40 p.m. Nikki and Vincent Gialotti, Chief of Surgery await outside the double-doors of the emergency entrance. He climbs out and rushes to her. *She'd arrived earlier to ensure the operating room had all necessary equipment and that the right surgical team was assembled.* He notices her expression's one of uncommon worriment! *He knew her and Jonathan had been social, but had no idea as to the degree!* She's rattled! "How's he doing, Nik?" "Well, his vitals still haven't stabilized! It was risky inducing the coma! But it was the only option!" *He nods.* "Where can I review the images and plan the procedure?" Before she's a chance to answer Gialotti interrupts offering his hand, "Dr. Oka, it's my honor to meet you! I'm Vincent Gialotti, Chief of surgery. My office's at your disposal." *He doesn't smile and dismisses the man's hand. His mind's on his brother!* "Thank-you, Doctor. Can we go now?" he challenges curtly! Gialotti turns, pushes the doors open and hurriedly leads them to his office! He and Nikki plot their surgical strategy and go over each step. He also makes an unusual request of her! After they've finely tuned the surgical timetable she leaves to prep herself, fulfill his request and brief the assisting team. Nikki and Ko are excellent surgeons and an amazing team! Jeff Rahdiya, photographer from the Dailey News is on the scene because of an unrelated shooting incident and witnesses the meeting! He recognizes Ko and snaps a few pictures!

4:24 p.m. The observation deck of the surgical theatre's filled to capacity! Everyone's heard of him, but none here have witnessed him at work!

4:25 p.m. He enters the operating room and observes sleeping Jonathan for a few measured moments. It's almost as if he's communicating with him! He'll do all he can for him…his best! He observes the readings of the monitoring devices, while Nikki inconspicuously adds the contents of the ampoule to the IV drip.

4:29 p.m. She takes her position beside him.

4:30 p.m. He picks up the surgical saw. Pushes the button…the buzzing begins. Minute chips of flesh and bone fleck into the air.

4:33 p.m. The buzzing ceases. Cautiously he removes the small piece of skull, roughly the diameter of a nickel, he'd meticulously cut and sets it inside a petri dish containing sterile water. He then dispatches Nikki to collect the items he'd requested of her earlier; 25 cc's of fresh amniotic fluid and a 4x4 cm. section of placenta from a newborn Tauri.

4:35 p.m. He extracts the bullet.

4:41 p.m. She returns with the specimens.

4:49 p.m. He begins packing the hole gingerly with small pieces of the placenta that she'd painstakingly diced per his instruction. Then bathes the area with the amniotic fluid belonging to the placenta. With a larger intact section of it he covers the area of repair and delicately sutures it in place. When he's through he bathes the area once more and sops up the excess with sterile napkins. All vitals are good and strong!

5:09 p.m. As they carefully bandage his head he notices a tear welling in the corner of her eye and softly whispers, "He's going to be fine! No worries!" His eyes shift to the anesthetist and hers meet his. She gestures a positive nod. Her smile's hidden by the mask! Once more he observes the read-outs of the life supporting devices. Lastly, he looks about the room to the team. Although his smile's hidden, his voice clearly exudes joy and gratitude as he praises, "Good work! Well done! Thank-you! Thank-you so very much!" *Applause fills the observation deck!* He places his hand on sleeping Jonathan's and bends to his ear, "All will be well my brother! No worries!"

5:11 p.m. Jonathan's wheeled into recovery! NOT intensive care!

He returns to Gialotti's office to unwind and moves to the coffee maker. As he's about to pour a cup he notices a small envelope addressed to him propped up against its base. He picks it up and retrieves the note inside. It informs that the garment bag and small duffel in the scarlet leather chair are for him and that transport will pick him up from the loading dock at 7:50 p.m. Now he can refresh and re-dress before his final examination.

6:00 p.m. Refreshed and re-dressed he finally prepares a cup of coffee and calls Nate to report.

6:35 p.m. He returns to Jonathan's bedside, checks his vitals and takes a seat intended for family members and friends to observe him.

7:15 p.m. He rises to check him once more. All signs are positive. He bends to his ear for the last time, "All's well 'J'!" *He doesn't see Jonathan's finger tap twice!*

After informing Gialotti of suggestive treatment he signs the necessary forms transferring Jonathan's care to his authority. Gialotti extends his hand once again. This time he accepts. "Dr. Oka, it's been a pleasure to watch you work! And your use of the placenta and amniotic fluid was pure genius! I'd like to discuss it more with you sometime!" "I'd like that very much!" he returns with a partial smile before walking away.

7:48 p.m.

Ko stands on the loading dock with the duffel slung over his shoulder and garment bag in hand as the Ghost pulls up. Byron climbs out, "Good-evening, Doc! Success?" "Yes!" Byron nods acknowledgement and proceeds to relieve him of his bags. Then climbs into the driver's seat! They arrive to the corporate hangar at 8:29 p.m. The pilot lifts-off at 8:36 p.m. Destination 'Angel Place' to pick up another passenger before proceeding to the final destination, 'Locus Angeli'.

As Ko'd slept during the flight to Philadelphia various procedures had entered his mind like a summer breeze.

CHAPTER TWELVE
inĐoctrination
anĐ seĐuction

MAY 10TH
12:30 p.m.

As the last of them steps into the cabana a Midnight Express 43 Open speeds toward them. Its helmsman cuts the engine fifteen feet away from the shore, coasts into the shallows and moors. The barefooted boatsman jumps into the water and sprints toward them beckoning excitedly, "Come! Come!" Without hesitation they remove their footwear, wade to the boat and climb aboard.

Twenty minutes later, less than twenty feet away from what had appeared a small vessel on the horizon is '*Scherazade*'! A breath-taking 418 meter mega luxury yacht! One of a kind! Once all are aboard *she* glides south effortlessly. They remain on deck absorbing the majesty of the view! It's truly an example of *Mother Nature* at *her* best! The chief officer, Francois smiles broadly as he moves to Doe and Nate, "Welcome! Welcome! Welcome aboard! You're a sight for sore eyes! *Scherazade*, the crew and I've missed you!" he hails while extending his hand to him. They shake and man-hug! "I know! And believe me! We've missed *her* and all of you too!" Nate returns enthusiastically. Doe delivers a cold flirtatious glance to him, "Is that the best welcome you can offer?" He moves to her, embraces her affectionately and 'air' kisses each cheek! Claire and the others watch wondering whether their exchange's beyond platonic!

Francois's six feet, seven inches has a great physique, enchanting eyes and a heart melting baritone, Swedish accented voice that's easy as a glass of water to drink in! In his uniform he's big girl candy! *'What a treat he'd be to unwrap!' Is the prevailing thought between Jae and Claire!* He greets them, as well as, Michael and Hakeem, "Good-morning!" After exchanging introductions and pleasantries he informs, "Ladies, the 'Althea's' prepared for you and gentlemen the 'MLK's' prepared for you!" Claire looks to Jae, "Come on! Let's check out our quarters!" "I'd like to see ours too! Come on!" chides Hakeem. Francois directs their way.

Each cabin easily sleeps six comfortably with a king, queen and two double-beds, a fully stocked 'wet' bar, two full baths, three showers, a sitting room with leather sofa, two comfy chairs and two recliners. The women and Hakeem are taken aback by the opulence! *Michael's familiar with the vessel and her crew!* Francois stands at the cabin's entrance watching Claire and Jae inspect it like excited little girls would a new doll house! Doe notices him watching and questions with raised eyebrow, "Francois?" "Uh…uh I just wanted to ask if Jae or any of you would like to ski? The weather's perfect and the water's calm!" "Um hmp!" she smiles. She looks to Jae, "Do you ride?" Jae's looks to her a tad confused! Doe probes further, "Jet ski…jet ski! Do you jet ski?" She shakes her head negatively. "Well! Want to try? Claire you ride right?" "Oh yes!" "Come on Jae! You'll like it! And you couldn't be in safer hands! Plus, we'll be together! What'd ya say?" Claire coaxes. "Uhhh…okay." Jae surrenders nervously. "Great! We'll meet in the garage. Say twenty minutes?" suggests Doe. "That'll be perfect!" he replies holding Jae in his gaze. *The D.O.O., Tamesh and Mobahi had thought of everything to pamper them and keep them at ease as they progressed thru conversion. The greater the peace within them the more accelerated the affect and the sooner they'll realize what and who they are!*

Francois's releasing a ski from its storage space as they enter. Jae's momentarily frozen by the sight of him! Atlas biceps, brawny thighs, rippling abs and pleasingly plump tush! He's striking to say the least! And she's blazing too! *Claire and Doe snicker at their captivation with each other!* "The girl's been bitten!" Claire whispers. "Him too!" smirks Doe as Hakeem and Michael enter. Claire interrupts, "Uh…um! Can we suit up now?" *They blush back to the moment!* After donning wet suits they mount up and skip across the water laughing and joking back and forth! The only exception… Jae! She's clinging to Francois like saran wrap! Her grip eases significantly after half an hour. He idles the ski to check the time…3:46 p.m. Then signals to the others and they race back.

A few feet away from the vessel they decelerate, coast in and surrender their 'skis' to waiting crewmen for cleaning and storage. Doe's last. As she rejoins the group she glances to a smiling Jae! "Well! Was it fun?" "Yes! Thank-you for pushing me! I never would've done it on my own!" she offers excitedly! Doe nods with a smile, "You're very welcome!" "Listen! I don't know about anyone else, but I'm going to refresh and just relax a bit before cocktails." Hakeem remarks. Nate nods, "That's a good idea for everybody!"

Doe and Nate seek the privacy of their personal cabins, circular-shaped, transparent units with the added feature of retractable ceilings that open to the stars, on the third deck. They sleep among the others, but for the time being use their own facilities for relief and refreshing. *The conversion of their bodies is further advanced and they don't want to alarm them!*

Jae awakes from a short nap before the others, refreshes and goes to the 'Park' to watch the sunset. *The 'Park's an area of manicured grass, miniature palm and hibiscus trees, rubber plants and custom-made furniture on the first deck at the aft of the vessel.* She's leaning on the guard railing looking across the water to the horizon when the others and Francois arrive. He moves to where Doe stands, "I just wanted to thank-you! I really enjoyed all of you! It was fun, but duty calls!" "Oh! It was a pleasure! I always have a good time with you! However, Claire and Jae enjoyed your company too! They really like you!" He blushes, excuses himself and goes over to Jae. Doe takes a seat beside Claire, but maintains a watchful eye as he leans on the railing next to her. "*She's* beautiful isn't *she*?" he whispers referring to the sun and all of *Earth's nature*! She turns her eyes to him and smiles, "Ooh! Yes! And so are you!" He returns her smile! "Jae, I just wanted you to know it's been a pleasure to meet you! I really had fun today!" Without warning he embraces her, kisses her cheek, releases her and walks away. Claire looks to Doe dumbfounded! "Did...did...did you see that? We didn't get that!" she snaps! "Hmmm...how about that!" Doe remarks sharply. In the blink of an eye, Claire's attention's diverted and transfixed! He's a bit taller than Francois, has a well-sculpted, sun baked body, beautiful eyes and pearly white teeth! The man's beyond eye candy! He's addictive! Before Doe can turn to see what's drawn her attention huge hands gently grab her shoulders! She feels the warmth of his breath on her neck and inhales his intoxicating scent as he bends and his lips caress her cheek. She smiles, turns and peers into his face, "Its o-o-h so good to see you, Pierre!" She stands and they hug tenderly for a long moment! Claire attempts to analyze what she's witnessing and Jae too! They release and she introduces, "Pierre, this is Claire Tamarumaro. Claire, this is Commodore Pierre DuQuois, Scherazade's skipper!" Claire extends her quivering hand and he lifts it to his lips, "The pleasure's all mine, Cherie!" *She's melting at the moment!* "I beg to differ!" she flirts. Jae has returned her attention to the sea. Nate glances to her and detects her somberness. He summons her, "Jae! Jae!" while gesturing to his side. She acknowledges and seats herself beside him. He looks into her eyes and his voice fills with concern. "What's wrong?" The others now cast their attention to the two of them! She begins to rave, "They're abusing, torturing *her* every day! Their acts are intentionally vile and fatal! They don't care! They lack compassion! They're the epitome of evil!" Gently he takes her hand and gazes into her eyes, "You're absolutely correct. Chaos, death, hardship and suffering are the elements that satisfy their souls and delights their black holes! They've no hearts! It's what they desire! It's who and what they are! The Bahleide are as poisonous trees and the BTs their fruits! Never will they change!" "Well! I'm weary of them treating *her* with no respect! And look what happened lately in the way they treated the Tauri feminine who spoke out against the sexually deviant light BT male they'd selected for the highest court in the land! I'm beyond frustrated with young Tauri girls being subjected to genital mutilation! I've tired of humanoid trafficking, enslavement and prostitution! Children and feminine being housed in cages like feral animals! Weary of BT males poisoning *Earth*! I'm just worn!" Her frustration's clear, deeply felt and shared! Nate glances to Doe. *She lowers her eyes in empathy.* Claire interjects. "I feel the same! But what really ticks me off is the mismanagement of the fresh water supply and bottled water! There shouldn't be a need for any being in North Americas not to drink the water from the faucet! Water should always be clean and safe! The only beings who should need bottled water are those in drought-stricken areas, areas of polluted water sources and in distant lands who've limited access to clean water, the 'Flint, Michigans' of the world! Also the use of plastics must be discontinued. It's caused and is causing devastating effects on sea life and the oceans!"

Hakeem can no longer hold his silence. "Well, I'm saddened by the crisis regarding physical, sexual abuse and trafficking of children and feminine! Too many have been and are being victimized! Too many children have died of starvation and others are starving! And the argument of abortion! I don't like the idea or reality of it! But that's truly an issue and circumstance that can only be judged by the Divine! Off-spring were meant to be a display and product of desire! Whoever creates the off-spring's responsible for its nurturing, education and meeting its needs! None other! If a female's either too young, a victim of rape, financially disadvantaged or the child is at risk in some manner or she's just not ready, I can understand the choice, albeit heart-wrenching! But a male has no right nor authority over feminine bodies nor their choices! That authority belongs only to the D.O.O! I don't see anyone volunteering robust support, financial, physical or structural to adopt the unwanted souls and treat them with compassion and love, building orphanages or donating funds for their care! Even in the distant past when there were institutions for the unwanted they were often victims of abuse and murder! And another thing! The feminine are the superior and for males to intentionally deprive them of knowledge, education and a seat at the head of every table's disgusting and wrong!" declares Hakeem. *Michael and Nate nod in agreement!*

"We understand your frustrations! A few weeks ago Doe received an invitation from Vaughn Burtron to accompany him on an ecological investigative tour of Bangladesh. What they discovered and witnessed was an appalling state of de-forestation! Sadly, it's one of many environmental tragedies occurring around the world at a 'pants on fire' scale' that too many of the world's populous aren't even aware of! They don't even understand the implications of the most recent reports on a layman's level! Because they know little about the planet on which they live! And it's not their fault because they were never told! Never allowed to know! I get peeved every time I think about their refusal to heed the past and present warnings of the tribal peoples around the world! And how they intentionally close their minds and cover their eyes for the sole purpose of greed and deny others the fullness of knowledge! Even now they turn a blind eye and deaf ears to those *small* voices, around the world crying out in defense of *Earth*. If only there'd been a way for them (Tauri) to have gained access to the *Compendium* all would be so very different! Life would be utopian! *She'd* be healthy and vibrant! The feminine would be in total governance and all would be disciplined, harmonious and the population balanced thru out the world!" states Nate solemnly.

Doe can no longer hold her silence, "I'm as concerned as all of you and the world for the Tauri of North Americas regarding the orange-haired, deranged, egotistical, bigoted, politically ignorant, mentally deficient, despicable madman that occupies the People's House and is surrounded by other *elephants* who, like him, lack moral character, decency, compassion and are gas lighting hate and discord while intentionally ignoring injustice, loss of life and treasure! *Kujoe's* in the 'House' and the *elephants* would lead all to believe its *Lassie*! They're an imminent danger! It really burns my derriere to hear the radical, right-wing rage about taking *their* country back! It's a joke! They're living in a fantasy that's lasted far too long!

It's time to awake the Tauri to the truth! The Americas were never BT ancestral lands! They spew falsehoods and vitriol about immigrants of whom they and their generations were and are a part! They invaded the Americas! They weren't invited! Factually and technically speaking *they* should be the ones vacating! Returning to their cold, rugged undesirable places of ancestral *seeding*! They've No Right to Be Here! Yet, they'd demand a wall built to deny women and children of coloration, Tauri, refuge from conditions of certain murder, rape or starvation! Had the natives of this land, in the past, been as soulless they'd have exterminated the first of them *(light' BT invaders)* to deter all others from following! But despite their cruelty and vileness the Tauri allowed them to remain and even helped them to survive! The dark ones even cooked their food, reared their children and suckled their young! They were of a finer fabric, a different breed! It's still difficult to understand why light BT males light keep castigating the Tauri as the evil in society? When it's them who terrorize not only the colorful, but their own! They're the ones with the hate groups! The majority of murders and other crimes are committed by them! They're defiling places of peace! Places of worship …churches, mosques and synagogues! Early prisons were built for 'light' BTs! Those of coloration in times past were too terrified to commit crimes! Plus, they were already being enslaved, terrorized, murdered and unjustly imprisoned by them! In the past the dark ones sought to gain justice thru peaceful demonstration some who protested bore legal arms, the *Panthers*. Their mission was to improved conditions for school age children in the community. They started free breakfasts, pantries and killed no one! But were casts as the 'demons' by the toxic 'light' BTs! How odd is it that they seek the comfort of colorful natives of island nations and countries of warm climates, beautiful waters and pristine beaches for enjoyment, pleasure and relaxation, but on the other hand declare the same dark skinned people to be the evil of the world? And why is there no mention of the countless Europeans and other non-dark that come thru the airports and sea ports of New York and Californias or cross the borders, official and unofficial, of Canada every day? Or those who overstay their visas! If truly tracked and counted their numbers would prove to be far greater than those at the southern border! Everyone's being distracted! It's madness! However, one day the Tauri of the world will awaken to the naked, mind-shattering truth that they've been living a false reality for more than 3,000 years! They'll wake-up to the fact that *Earth's* a living being! They'll discover, understand and accept that the feminine are the superior! But most importantly they'll learn that there exists something more defining between each than race! Something even their brightest minds have yet to discover!"

The sky darkens, tumultuous gray clouds roll in and wind driven rain begins sprinkling onto the 'Park'. *Doe looks to the sky.* "I suggest we move to the 'Cloud'." *A lounge/kitchen combo space.* Within seconds of her suggestion the deluge begins. Once inside they raid the containers of food and desserts in the refrigerator, prepared by Petra, Jamie and Max. Mano had ordered their delivery to the ship earlier. After satisfying their hunger they clean-up their mess, bid Doe, Nate and each other 'well'! *Passion fruit drinks await them.*

After a few moments Doe and Nate look about the room. It's empty. The *seedlings* are gone. *She sighs heavily.* "Nate! Did you feel the weight of their empathy and sadness?" He cocks his head slightly to the side and grimaces a bit before looking directly into her oculi. "Yes. Strangely, it was distressing, exhilarating and mournful all at once! Their KSCs are clearly opening! But their ability to actually feel *her* pain's growing faster than we anticipated! Especially in Jae! It's time we told them!" "I know! But Nate! How do we deliver the news we have for them?" *He exhales deeply*! "Well... fortunately they're in the process of conversion. Thanks to your insight the impact will be minimal!" *She gives him a concerning glance!* "Is there nothing we can do for *Earth,* the *Tauri,* before we return home?" he probes. *She shakes her head contemplatively.* "Nate! The Prime Directive's still in place! There've been no breaches of its terms!" "I know! Doe! I'm not talking about turning the world upside down! Just something to 'highly' motivate BTs to cease their aggressive harassment, murder and oppression of them. To stay away from them! To keep their claws off of them!" "Hmmm? Maybe! Maybe, there're some small tactics we can employ!" They look to each other with mischievous smiles! "Nate! I'm going to rest and think on this further! Tomorrow we'll define our actions, after we 'tell' them!" He rises, pauses briefly and sighs with a smile, "Okay! I bid you good-night! Be well!" Pierre enters as they're preparing to retire and alerts them of an incoming communication! Without delay they make their way to the 'Consilium'.

They enter and move to the four foot tall column at the midst of the room. It's a glassy surface encircled with embedded mini indicator lights which are unlit. Slowly she waves her hand over them. The lights begin to flicker and stabilize to full illumination. Within seconds four dimen-sional holographic images of Tamesh and Mobahi appear before them and they're smiling! "Congratulations on your success! Your accomplishment's wonderful!" They bow their heads in humble gratitude! Immediately Doe begins to implore, "Please forgive me for contacting Jonas first! But--" Tamesh raises her hand in a halting position! "It's fine! It was the right decision, Commander! The report's been sent and we're awaiting instruc-tions and orders for departure! We'll all be returning home very soon!" she comments with exaggerated delight! "Umm…about returning home! How long will it take for transport to arrive?" Nate queries. Mobahi chuckles, "I knew you'd be the one to inquire! Uhh…best estimate three or four years. So tell us! How're they doing?" "From all observations and indications they're adjusting perfectly!" "Good! Anything further either of you want to inform us of?" Tamesh probes. Doe looks to Nate who's equally baffled by her inquiry! "Uhh…no!" they answer. The *keepers* smile to each other with a *knowing*! "Please seat yourselves." *They comply.* She continues, "Your success has triggered the activation of the 'SROAT' and your powers have been restored! Of course, no killing! There're worse conditions that can be invoked! There's a provision hidden deep in the sub-text of the centuries old 'Agreement' between the *D.O.O.* and the Bahleide that even we weren't aware of until the ORS informed us! All of you are granted full authority to commence the re-conditioning campaign with special priority given to the feminine and children first! *She pauses and smiles broadly!*

I must say the two of you look happier than ever and it's pleasing to see! Now, you've much to plan and execute! Again well done! The village sends their love! We're all so very proud of you!" They smile and bow their heads reverently. "This is great news! Thank-you! We're grateful! But this news couldn't have come at a better time! The Bahleide are aware of something! *She pauses and realizes, in that moment, that they're sensing the seedlings! They know they're upon Earth! They just don't know where! However, this time we can protect the Tauri! This time we can stop them! This time we've the opportunity to set things to correct order!* The 'keepers' look one to the other then nod to her. "Yes, Commander! Your thoughts are accurate. Now be well! Have no fear! *They'd heard her thoughts!* Oh! And please tell Jae the cages are a *go!*" *Their images dissipate! Doe and Nate look to each other confused by her message for Jae. They don't recall Jae ever mentioning cages! Much less speaking directly with Tah! They've not yet met!* "Nate! I must confess! Since meeting and sharing with them I've experienced peace and joy equal only to our last Christmas with Uncle Kaseem! Even my slumber's more restorative!" "I know! I share your experience and it's wonderful! They'd expressed a strong desired to aid the *Tauri!* They'll be pleased to learn we've full authority to do just that! We're going to 'play' (*formulate and strategize*) as a team, a family! Together we'll protect and save the extended members of our bonah!" "But Nate we must tell them!" "Doe! You worry for naught! They're human! Not humanoid! They'll be just fine!"

Sunday May 11th

Day Four

They sleep late thru no fault of their own! Ko's first to awake in the 'MLK' cabin. Hakeem *feels* his presence, raises his head and squints about. "Ko?" he queries groggily. "Yes, Keem! It's me! Sssh!" Hakeem returns his head to the pillow and Ko proceeds to the bathroom. Minutes later, when Nate enters he's dressed and groomed. "P-s-s-t! Ko! Come! Come! I want to show you about!"

Ko, Nate and Mano are conversing over breakfast juices when Claire and Jae enter the 'Cloud'. They're surprised to see him! He notices their astonishment and smiles! "Awww...come on now! Did you really think I wouldn't return! That I'd miss the remainder of our stay and the fun?" They look to each other, "Honestly, we were uncertain! You left so fast!" Jae replies. Claire queries. "Well? Were you able to save the patient?" "Yes. All's well!" Extremely bubbly Doe enters with Angela by her side, "Good-morning everyone!" she chirps! Claire bursts with laughter! "Whoa! This is really going to rock his world! I can't wait to see his face!" The others join her laughter! Claire and Jae move to Angela with questions. She explains that Doe had contacted her midday on Friday and invited her to spend the week-end. She'd accepted and would've arrived sooner if it hadn't been for the emergency. In the meantime, Doe seats herself between Ko and Nate. Gently she nudges Ko with her shoulder and whispers, "You're amazing! I'm glad you're back!" *They smile to each other! Doe detects a strong, familiar scent emanating from him and glances to Nate. He smiles with a nod!*

When he and Michael enter Hakeem stops dead in his tracks at the sight of her! Overjoyed he looks to Doe and moves to Angela. "How are you? I mean...I mean...I'm glad you're here!" She smiles, "I'm glad too!" *They've been like magnets ever since meeting at the reception.* Hakeem walks over to Doe, leans to her and whispers, "Thank-you, Commander!" "You're more than welcome!"

98

After they've cleaned-up the mess from breakfast Hakeem announces, "I'd like to take Angela and Ko skiing! Anybody want to join us?" "Sure! We're down!" replies Michael and Doe. "Yeah! Me too!" adds Jae! Doe executes a double-take! "Are you sure?" "Yeah, I'm not afraid anymore!" "I know that's right!" Doe quips! "Can Francois come?" Jae requests. "Why of course! I'll arrange it! Claire you're not coming?" Doe queries. "No. I'd really like to play a calming game of chess." She's surprised by her answer! "You play?" "Yeah! I'm not a savant! I just enjoy the game!" "Well, my dear! I have the perfect player for you!" Doe looks at him, "Nate, did you set this up?" He smiles, "No! But I'd be more than delighted to play with her!" *Doe gives him a glance, 'Hump! I know you will!* "Well! They're going to be lost to us for a while. We'd better get a move on!" she suggests to the others. *During his conversations with Jae he'd learned that Claire played chess. But he'd been too shy to challenge her to a game!*

They ride the waves for a couple of hours. When they return to Scherazade they check on the players. They're still engaged in the state of play! Michael announces, "I'm on my way to refresh before cocktails. See you then." The others follow his lead.

6:45 p.m.

Doe and Nate are puzzled as they await their arrival to the 'Cloud'! *They know the therapy's effective because they carry a scent! Yet, not one has mentioned any unusual occurrence!* Ko's last to enter. Nate looks to each sternly, "We know you've each experienced something out of the norm, because we can *smell* you!" Feigning ignorance Hakeem queries "That cotton candy aroma! What is it? Is it the two of you?" "No, Hakeem! That's us! You included!" Nate replies a tad impatient! The group looks to Doe and Nate and erupt with laughter! "We know who and what we are and we're aware of our scent! After all **we're human**! Doe reflects mentally with an inconspicuous smile! *'They're assimilating faster than anticipated!'* "Oh, well! Then you realize like us you're **first generation**!" *The silence's deafening!*

Nate pierces the vacuum. "Doe and I were informed very early this morning by the *keepers* about *specialties* attached to our success in your location! Specialties they've only learned of! First…all of us have earned the restoration of our powers and authority. We'll assist you with their application. Secondly, our actions have activated the SROAT and commencement of its operations; #1- Re-conditioning of the Tauri. Prepping *Earth* for renewal and the restoration of *her daughters* to power! Now we can formulate a plan and take action to help protect them!" *They look to each other with smiles of pure joy!* We've approximately thirty-six or forty-eight months before our transport arrives. That's more than enough time for us to accomplish the necessary changes to allow them to re-boot society." *Images of methods, strategies and new knowledge begin to stream thru their 'ccs', central concept stimulators!*

They relocate to the 'Consilium'. A situation room, equipped with devices unknown to present technology. Doe's enters the room first and generates a 4-D holographic image of a planet slowly rotating mid-air. As they enter their attention's drawn to it and they gather about it like children viewing an eye-catching exhibit on a field trip! It's an awesome sight! It's young *Earth! Her* landmass is solid, absent fragmentation with spiney rivers, countless lakes, ponds and five huge oceans! "Look closer!" she invites. As they concentrate they're able to envision *her* with present day overview grid imagery and are taken aback by the dramatic changes they see! There're now four oceans versus five! Despite *her* violent eruptions and quakes *she'd* provided natural barriers to the north of Africa, Europe, Turkey and Saudi Arabia in an attempt to protect the places of *her children!* Likewise to the southeast and west *she's* separated to create islands, Australia, Fiji, the Philippines, Samoa, Formosa, Hawaii, Bermuda, New Zealand, West Indies and the Caribbean islands. *Her children* are the natives of these rich, tropical, remote moderate temperature places. Commander Doe looks about them, "It's time for correction. Many are confused and question why there's so much turmoil! But the answer's a simple one! The *Earth's* out of balance! The Tauri are worn of 'light' BT rule especially in North Americas, but also BT rule around the globe! Native Tauri, shall have the land of North Americas returned to their full authority and resume their responsibility of protecting *her heart*! It's time for BTs to leave the lands they've invaded, Australia, North and South Americas, Hawaiian Islands, Alaska, Canada and New Zealand. They've proven they cannot live in peace! BTs must return to their ancestral places! *She exhales.* Okay! It's time to decide what we want to do! How we want to do it? And where to start?" Jae interjects, "Hmm, there's the Russian, Korean, Chinese, Japanese, African and South Americas despots who're direct threats to the advancement of society and detrimental to peace on *Earth*!" "I know, Jae! We're delaying revenge on them!" Ko interjects, "Hey! Don't you think it fitting to concentrate on the males first? After all, they're responsible for the damages of the past and present? We can address the corrupt BT feminine later! Right now the males should be the targets!" Michael nods agreement. "Sounds good to me! You've definitely got my vote! Especially after the performance of the old, bigoted 'light' BT senators who disrespected Drs. Fjord and Hillser in such a loathing manner! Neither of the Tauri feminine were lying, regarding the vulgar males whom they'd filed official complaints against! All immoral BT males need to be taught a lesson!" The feminine look to each other and smile broadly, "You know guys? We're with you!" Doe moves to the console, "How about some inspirational rhythms while we work?" After pushing a few buttons an extended remake of 'Change the World' by Eric Clapton floods the audio. They pull chairs up to the indented spaces of the desk-like fixture that runs against the length of the west wall and begin operating the advanced devices as if second nature. *The therapy's definitely effective.* As they move their digits and hands holographic four dimensional images of symbols, text, numeric equations appear mid-air before them and remain suspended as if attached to an invisible blackboard! Their input generates new algorithms, equations and formulations that appear and stream modify. *Their primary targets are devices and activities that harm Earth and society!*

Six immediate goals are agreed upon:

#1- stimulate the opening of the knowledge storage cells in the thalamus located in the diencephalon area of Tauri brains to awaken them to their true identities via reinforcement of knowledge offered at 'KFs' (Knowledge Forums).

#2-destruction of firearms, munitions, their manufacturers, storage places as well as retail stores.

#3 - halting the abusive practices against *her* i.e. drilling and use of explosives.

#4- ending the violence against Tauri women, young girls, children and males.

#5- the cleansing of Africa, the ancestral place of *'Tauri seeding'*

#6- Sentinels are dispatched from the Plantation to the Wicatah reservation to assist with the rebuilding of the *Nation.*

#7- destruction of all casinos foreign and domestic

They summon Jonas into their midst via 'vc' for assistance, collaboration and to strategize. *Commodore DuQuois reverses course.*

By 3:43 a.m. their strategies, applications and formulations are completed. Jonas activates the sentinels into active mission status and the *'Plantation's'* placed on high alert! Jonas, the *seedlings*, Doe and Nate bid each other 'well'.

At 5:49 a.m. production of the various formulas goes into high gear with utmost precision in the laboratories of the research and development departments at the 'PGG' base in Michigan and the 'Institute of Science and Technology' at the Greenwood.

Due to the time of year conditions couldn't be more perfect for the implementation of their strategies. The weather's warming, people are out and about and it'll soon be summer! Amusement parks will teem with people vacationing from places near and far, national and foreign. There'll be an abundance of indoor and outdoor activities and events. In the heat of the day free ice cream, popsicles, water ice and tasty treats will be temptations hard to resist!

The *Auton's* a multi-tiered weaponized drug. Within it are markers, placed there by the D.O.O. that trigger various physiological and or physical transfigurations. A true example of advanced technology marrying bio-chemistry, nano-genetic reconstruction and synthetic frequency receptors.

The Plantation's, one of two training facilities constructed long ago. It's located on an island, a bit smaller than the state of Delaware, inside the Bermuda Triangle.

Knowledge Forums

Abandoned motels, strip malls, warehouses and commercial buildings are converted seemingly overnight! Hours of operation are 9 a.m.-9 p.m. seven days a week and their doors open promptly at 9:00 a.m. Each has an enormous teardrop-shaped room with tiered stadium seating. This room's for assemblies and referred to as the 'Centre'. All facilities are set-up identically with monitor stations, free cafés, library areas of books and other printed materials, restrooms, showers and child care facilities. At this place the feminine will re-discover and nurture their power. Males will discover the superiority of the feminine and a new level of respect for them. The majority of the populous is ignorant to the political process and its function from the local to national level. This is by intention and was implemented during the *elephant's* reign of governance in the latter part of the 1970's. The 'KFs' will solve this handicap and many others! Political changes will occur during the upcoming election! The feminine will regain their dominance and the world will become a more eco-friendly, peaceful place! They'll be no second term for Kujoe! He shouldn't have had a first! But this time will be different! This time they'll be fully awake, informed and aware! Finally, they'll see him for the doofist monster he is! Finally they'll no longer believes his lies!

Tauri humanoids by majority don't fully grasp, understand the reality that **they are 'democracy'**! Socialism simply means for the good of the whole! It's not a threatening word to be whispered! The Tauri must understand that each of their votes are as accumulating grains of sand creating a mound or in this case the 'mountain of democracy'! Every citizen must awaken to the weight of their golden vote and the power of the money in their wallets! They must realize the two powers they possess! One's their vote and the other their money! How can corporations attain riches without patronage to their products? Every registered citizen must answer the call for the good of the whole!

The Tauri I.Q. levels have been deliberately retarded over the centuries by the Bahleide and enforced by the BTs. In concert with the 'auton' the 'KF's' will be an added measure to resolve this handicap! Finally the film over their 'mind's eyes' will be dissolved.

'The keepers remind them that it's their responsibility to inform the Tauri populous of the world as to who the Russian is that has so much influence and power over the mad ogre and directs havoc world-wide! They must help them to understand what the Russian is! Not who it appears to be! He's not a 'BT'! He's an actual Bahleide! He'd crafted the unrest and terror now occurring around the world many years ago! They were incremental parts of his much larger plan of world domination…KING!'

CHAPTER THIRTEEN
law enforcement

MONDAY MAY 12TH

8:12 a.m.

Federal Investigation Bureau, Harrisburg, Pennsylvania

Morrison's sipping a cup of coffee with one hand and reading a report with the other when they knock on his door. He beckons them. "Good-morning, sir!" Grayson greets as he offers their report. "I don't know about it being a 'good' morning! D.C.'s breathing down our necks for answers!" Morrison grumbles while gesturing them to sit.

After a few minutes he lays the report on the desk and gives them a concerning look, "Do we have the vehicle?" "Yes, sir. The forensic team's processing it as we speak!" Morrison shakes his head in frustration, "We're missing something! Same vehicle, number of actors and apparel. There's got to be a connection! Oh! What's this about piles of an unknown substance at the site? Is it drugs?" Grayson glances to Deevers, "Sir, by the time we arrived at the scene the victims had been taken to the hospital and the haz-mat team had completed the clean-up and were leaving the scene. But the stench of the stuff hung in the air! Sir, it smelled worse than rotting flesh!" *Morrison grimaces.* "And these two men, Bryce and Lucien?" "Sir they check out clean as a whistle! They're outstanding, law abiding citizens! They don't even have parking tickets! They're single and no they're not gay! They're dedicated to helping the boys stay out of trouble, prison and alive! They've been mentoring a drafting/architectural design workshop for inner city kids out of their own pockets, during the week-ends! They've helped all the young men/young ladies who've participated in their workshops achieve degrees! They address them as 'princes/princesses'. It's their way of reinforcing pride and respect. Their success rate's astounding! The young people have a special respect and affection for them! But sir! You should've seen and heard these kids! I mean young gentlemen! It's hard to believe they've come from the chaotic city streets, bruised families and down-trodden projects! Sir, they were extremely well-groomed, mannerly and articulate despite their circumstances! Notwithstanding the degree of shock they'd experienced, they maintained their composure! When you spoke with any of them it was very apparent that someone had spent quality time with them! Sir, these men are doing a phenomenal service in the community. It's baffling how they've transformed so many!" states Grayson. "Hmmm…are these black kids?" "Yes, some are! But they look more like the United Nations!" Deevers replies. "Okay! So why would anyone attack that office or those people? You think this was a botched hit? Wrong address? Wrong people?" Morrison probes. "Grayson and I think that's exactly what happened! These people were just unfortunate victims, not the targets! With that as a working theory, what and who was the intended target? And why? Hopefully, we'll learn more on Friday during the video conference with the Philly guys. In the meantime we'll wait on the lab results." "Good work!" Morrison compliments as they exit. He sits perplexed! *'Who'd called the haz-mat team?' He ponders whether he should give McCleery a consulting call. After a moment he shrugs off the idea.*

CHAPTER FOURTEEN
arrival, indoctrination and seduction

cont

MONDAY MAY 12TH
Day Five
They return to shore just before sunrise and seek the solace of their suites.
11:12 a.m.

Claire, Hakeem and Jae enter the 'Mango Room'. "Hey Mano! What's going on with the pyramids?" *She's referring to a table that has no service, but four, ten inch tall pyramids created of varying size white drawstring bags neatly stacked.* He looks to her and smiles, "I'm as much in the dark as you!" Jae gives a yielding hunch of her shoulders! Claire chuckles, "Nice try, J!" Hakeem's still chuckling as they seat themselves and bid Mano good-morning! "What do you suggest today?" "Hakeem! It's by request that everyone enjoy a 'Lotus' this morning!" They look to each other baffled and Claire probes! "What's that?" "It's Doe's original recipe! Served only in her presence. Today she honors you!" "Well bring it on! If it's her recipe it's gotta be good!" They're sipping on their drinks when Doe and Nate enter. *She's holding an envelope.* Hakeem spins around on his stool and smiles to her, "G-o-o-d-m-o-r-n-i-n-g gorgeous! This is an excellent recipe! You must tell me its secrets! Seems Mano's sworn to secrecy, lest he lose his head!" *The bar erupts into laughter!* Doe chuckles and shakes her head, "Just what am I going to do about you?" She moves to the gift laden table and gestures, "Come!" *She remains standing.* "I spoke with Jonas earlier and all's proceeding on schedule. Shipments begin on Saturday and preparations for the second phase are in progress. Tomorrow when you arrive home you'll be met by and acquainted with your 'neubas'. Claire and Jae since you live in such close proximity Angela will escort the two of you and introduce you. From that point on your 'neuba' will bring you up to speed! Ko! Michael will be your escort. Hakeem, Nate will be with you. Upon your return you'll be guarded around the clock. Your freedom's neither being interrupted nor restricted! You're just being protected! Keeping you safe's of the highest priority. We can't return home without each other!" She opens the small envelope she's been holding and withdraws four credit cards embossed with the Greenwood insignia and their names. She gives each one. *They've never ever seen anything like them!* "They've no limit and can be used anywhere! If the merchant challenges them, because they're rarely seen, just insist that he/she run it. Also funds have been added to your bank accounts. Nothing will stand in the way of your desires, needs or requests!" *Her voice fills with, for her, uncommon emotion!* "I want each of you to know that the days we've shared have been beyond pleasure! I know you must return to your homes. So we'll resign to looking forward to your return." *Everyone's contemplative.* Claire looks directly at Doe then to Nate, "Well! It's a two lane highway you know! WE shall miss the two of you also! You've provided us the elements to open our knowledge centers! You've awakened us to what and who we are! You've completed us and we're grateful! But we've a task at hand! The opportunity to minimize pain, misery and death for so many and little time before we leave! So let's buck up! Snap out of it!" she demands in a tone none have ever heard! It's the tone of command! Doe raises back a bit and comments, "Well! With that being said, please open the top bag."

Each reaches in and withdraws an unusual bracelet. It's comprised of wafer-thin, titanium-like tiles with the Greenwood insignia deeply etched at its midst. "They're weaponized communication devices, vital signs monitors and contain tracking elements. Once it's clasped on your wrist it becomes a seamless band! It's waterproof, shock-proof, unbreakable and useless to any other. Its trait specific to each of you! If for some reason you should ever have to use each other's it will respond." she instructs. After thoroughly demonstrating its operation, usage and capabilities the second bags are opened. Ko withdraws a pair of sunglasses that're quite stylish, but far from ordinary! "Whoa! These are way cool!" he comments! They've accu-sight, heat sensory, night vision qualities and a feature more defining than x-ray imagery! They're beyond binoculars! They uniquely semi-wrap around and adhere to the face! They're also laser enabled. Doe and Nate insist all move to the cabana before opening the last bag.

Once they've arrived she announces, "The garment inside's very special! We request you never take it off while you're away from your residences, as well as the chain about your neck. We refer to the garment as the ultimate skeleton or US. Nothing can penetrate it. It maintains your core body temperature and is indestructible. It also guards against skeletal damage due to impact. Now go try it on!" she urges enthusiastically! They hurry to the changing rooms.

Infectious, uncontrollable laughter erupts from both dressing rooms causing Doe and Nate to burst into laughter too! "Hey y'all! Doe and Nate got jokes!" Hakeem hollers over the partitions. The laughter's directed at the garment. It resembles Denton pajamas! *A one piece pajama garment designed for children back in the 50's.* Jae and Claire have begun to slip into their garments and are experiencing its unique quality. They look to one another in amazement and smile! It's beyond anything they've ever experienced! Claire hollers, "Hakeem, Ko! Calm down! Breathe! Then put it on!" Hakeem looks to him. They hunch their shoulders and stick a foot into a leg portion and work it gently down toward the toe section. As soon as the big toe nears its position the garment sucks it into place! Now they understand. After donning the garment they select swimwear from the drawers and emerge into the lounge. They look to one another shocked! It's invisible! All they see are swimsuits and skin! Doe and Nate have left the cabana and await them on the beach.

Their newly acquired swag's evident in their strides as they walk along the sand toward them. Jae and Claire are within arm's length of Doe when she queries, "Well? How does it feel?" Claire looks to Jae and they smile! "It feels extremely powerful! It feels good!" Jae replies. Claire nods agreement! Ko and Hakeem express the same sentiment to Nate!" "Excellent! All of you wear it well!" Nate compliments with a smile adding, "No one can use this garment other than yourselves. Now, Doe and I have a few matters to attend to, so we'll meet up later this evening! Let's say six in the Mango room. But please enjoy the day! Test your garments!" Jae's pensive and Doe takes notices, "What's wrong?" "Well, I'm not a swimmer really! I don't-" she interrupts, "Jae! Try the water." Something in her voice calmed Jae and quelled her fear. Doe and Nate begin walking back to their suites as the group looks to one another puzzled! "What do they mean, test it?" Ko queries. "I don't know! But I'm up for a quick dip!" says Claire. "Come on Jae! Ko and I will keep you safe!" promises Hakeem.

From Nate's balcony they observe them and share parental-like smiles of pride and gladness as they dive and glide!

An hour or so later the swimmers pause to survey around them. The shore's disappeared and they're more than two miles out! Oddly, they're neither winded nor panicked! Even Jae who was not a swimmer, swims like a fish! The group concludes their new skills are qualities provided by the US. But they're wrong! It's them!

Mango Room 6:00 p.m.

The *seedlings* are comfortably attired in casual evening dress, a bit chatty and completely unaware of the facial change that's occurred to their eyes as they enter the lounge! But it's a change the Beals detect immediately while sipping on Mai Tai drinks thru waxed paper straws from ripe cored pineapples. *Plastic straws are banned in their facilities and all of the Caribbean islands. It'll be the standard of the world very soon!* Doe and Nate glance one to another and smile! The *seedlings* seat themselves and look to them in silence! "Each of you've become spoiled brats!" she jests while signaling Mano to bring them pineapples too! Minutes later as they sip she taunts, "Everything better now?" "Sho' is!" blurts Jae mockingly! *All eyes in the room avert to the floor! Nate quickly interjects to cool the growing heat!* "Hakeem! What was it you were asking me earlier?" Hakeem looks to him understanding his cue, "Uh, let me think. But in the meantime, what can you tell us about the so-called 'space pigeons'? Are they real?" Nate casts a brief smile, "Oh, yes! They're real! They're GODADs. They sweep the void of space in search of vessels manned by crews of other lifeforms to commune with and guide to higher knowledge. Also the meaning of the rainbow's another lie! It isn't symbolic of a religious promise! It's an everlasting memorial to the green and violet Tauri who were hunted to extinction by the Bahleide and BTs! It's their spirits that today's younger generation has tapped into! However, the most devastating, diabolical tactic by the Bahleide was the concept of religion. It was genius! Nothing more than a form of control based on propaganda the Bahleide created and BTs collaborated and elaborated on. How insane and audacious of them to attempt to humanize the *Divine*! With each group claiming a different deity, which is the supreme among the earthly group? It's insanity! There's only one and that be the Divine Omnipotent One aka the D.O.O! The various Bahleide had little difficulty playing the role as 'gods'. Without their suits their bare countenance was grotesque enough for humanoids to consider them as something other! Another misconception they promoted was that the *Divine* required and demanded worship and praise! Nothing could be further from the truth! The D.O.O. isn't human and doesn't have that need!

The D.O.O.'s s-o-o-o-o beyond such a primitive mechanism! *They* only desired and desire the Tauri to function as they were intended. To care for *Earth*, live in peace, savor prosperity and reproduce according to the guideline provided in the 'Compendium'! But by seizing and hiding it the BTs forced the Tauri into a vortex of psychological falsehoods that far too many have had to accept and endure! We'll talk later about that! Right now! We know you've plans for the evening, because we do! Now go about your evening and be well!"

May 13th Day Six Departure

5:00 a.m.

He rises and performs his routine inspection of *her* via the 'corporate' surveillance system. *Her* condition continues to degrade. He heads to the bathroom to refresh. After dressing he walks the short distance down the corridor to her door and knocks softly. There's no answer. Certain she's there he knocks a little harder. Still no answer! Impulsively he turns the knob. The room's neat as a pin and the bed undisturbed! The 'cd' on the nightstand begins ringing and he answers, "Hello?" Her voice's solemn, "Good-morning, Nate. I'd a feeling you'd be there." "Where're you?" "I'm at Angel Place. Urgent matters dictated the necessity of my early departure. Plus, I didn't feel up to bidding them farewell." "What am I supposed to say to them?" "Nothing. I've left an envelope for them in a floral arrangement in the Atrium. All's in place, so don't worry and be well!" she bids.

He knew not only thru her actions, but by her voice that something wasn't right! Something was affecting her! She'd never had difficulty bidding farewell to anyone in the past! What was different now? He's no recourse other than to watch and wait! Regardless of the optics she's the feminine, thus his superior! He's no authority to question her, only the responsibility of concern.

As the group enter the café for breakfast it's apparent something's wrong! Only Mano's there to greet them! There's no Doe! No Nate! They'd greeted them every morning till now! Their absence surprises Mano too! Aware of their uneasiness he feigns distress in an attempt to lift their spirits. "Whoa! Oh no! What've you done with my high-spirited soulmates? Have you caused them harm?" *They're silent despite his effort to cheer them.* "Mano! Have you seen either of them this morning?" Claire probes. He looks to her, "No. Not yet! But come on, Claire! All of you! I've got mimosas prepared and the kitchen awaits your orders. I'm sure they'll be here soon!" He leaves the room to prepare offerings for breakfast because none would order! Claire, Jae, Hakeem and Ko look one to another baffled!

They've sipped on several mimosas and picked at the shrimp scampi and biscuits and gravy on their plates when Nate finally enters with an envelope in hand and alone! His demeanor's formal, versus casual, "Good-morning. I trust everyone slept well and is ready! I know you're wondering where's Doe, right?" He looks to Mano momentarily lowering his eyes as he hands the envelope to Hakeem, who's nearest to him. Hakeem accepts, pulls out the enclosed note and reads its message, 'Urgent matters demanded my immediate return to the estate. Will update you later this evening via your 'cd's'. Be well. Signed, D. B.' He's absent affect as he passes it to the others for review. Once all have read it Nate reminds, "Okay! The clock's ticking! We've got to get a move on!" Michael and Angela join their company and all exit the room.

At each destination they're met by their 'neubas', transported to their homes and introduced to their supporting security squads. Then taken on a tour to inspect the additional resources the 'Foundation's provided. Needless to say they're speechless!

It's late when their inspections are completed and they return to their residences. While preparing to retire their 'cds' signal. Its Doe and Nate confirming everything's in order and informing them of the latest updates.

In the morning they'll return to their workplaces, but it won't be business as usual! During the next few days, dependent upon their zone of responsibility, PGG members will seek their advisement and orders either in person or via telecommunications as they fully implement the campaign of the SROAT and begin the process of restoring the feminine to power.

CHAPTER FIFTEEN
αctivation of the sroat

Locus Angeli
MAY 14TH

Cotton ball clouds stretch across the turquoise sky and gentle trade-winds blow easing the humidity and heat of the day. *If only the world was like this once again!* Aircraft descend onto the palm tree lined tarmac every half hour delivering guests who've been summoned by Jonas. They're world renowned, highly respected experts in the fields of mathematics, quantum physics, medicine, psychology, philosophy, biology, chemistry and engineering of varying races and both sexes. It's a true 'rainbow' coalition and all are Tauri. On this day the intelligence agencies, NIA, FIB, AIA (Americas Intelligence Agency) and Interpol fail to detect the significance of regularities in the various travel arrangements of these distinguished individuals. *The one time they should've been diligent they're completely complacent and dysfunctional!* The last flight carrying Drs. Pierre Joliet and Erik Zahn touches down at 5:30 p.m.

A white linen envelope containing the itinerary for the weekend has been placed in the room of each guest. The first meeting's at 7:00 p.m. Participating faith-based leaders world-wide are brought into the meetings via the PGG's 'VCS' (visual audio communications system). *For reasons of security they were requested not to travel.*

Jonas Matthis was Kaseem Beal's first recruit and an integral part of the PGG's creation. He's bespectacled light blues eyes, salt and pepper hair and stands six feet, five inches and two hundred and thirty pounds. He's a brilliant mathematician and the product of a West Indian mother and Sicilian father, both of whom were Tauri. The strain in his mother was stronger than his father. At an early age he'd chosen to identify with his mother's people because they loved and respected *Earth* and enjoyed the celebration of *her* and life! Yet, the world beyond his own saw and mistakenly classified him as a 'light BT'! He's the 'keystone' of the 'SROAT'. Michael's voice had reeked of uncommon joy and excitement during that early morning call back in April when he'd requested him to create the *invitations*! Only a *seedling* could've invoked such a motivating spirit! Based on that alone Jonas green-lighted the program designated the 'SROAT' aka Societal Reconstruction of Tauri. A blue-print for enhanced intelligence programming of the Tauri.

The Planet Green Group aka 'PGG" are Tauri descendants. Present global membership stands just shy of two billion. An unbelievable communication network is in place! *During the early days (1800's) the foundation for the network had been laid and construction started. Jonas and Nate completed it with the installation and erection of the 'network globes'. Yesterday it came online without a glitch during testing! Upon inspection all components are dust and rust free after a little more than two centuries of dormancy!*

CHAPTER SIXTEEN
animal collection

MAY 15TH

PGG members descend on SPCAs and pet stores in specific states of North Americas and specific locations around the world posing as affluent couples with the sincerest of humane intentions and deep charitable pockets. They adopt and purchase as many canines and felines as possible without initiating any red flags, including birds and transport them to state of the art training centers aka ATCs.

The centers are 80x80 (twice the size of an average barn) climate-controlled and situated on a minimum of one hundred acres of woodlands located miles away from their point of procurement. The training rooms are larger than most elementary school gymnasiums. Directional indicators and detailed icons that adorn the floors appear freshly painted. *Kaseem Beal had purchased a considerable amount of land in the Americas (North and South) and around the world centuries ago in hopes it'd be of use to the SROAT someday!*

Upon arrival they're examined by teams of veterinarians and treated, if necessary. Then surrendered to groomers! When they're finished with them they pass each to a handler. The handler feeds them a meal containing a different composition of the 'auton' *(It contains an added 'evolutionary' boosting element and causes drowsiness.)* and water. *Sleep accelerates its affect.*

The animals and birds have always understood when spoken to!

Two days later at sunrise the animals and guardians awake. *Many of the handlers had slept on cots among them as part of the bonding process.*

They've been altered and have a cartilage-like organ that bears no resemblance to a larynx, but rather a grayish 'warm and serve' breakfast sausage! Now they can actually speak any language and be clearly understood!

As the massive Doberman stretches a strange long, deep sound resounds from his mouth he's never heard before! Likewise, as the sleek, shiny black Persian stretches she also lets out a sound unfamiliar to her ears! *They've yawned!* The Doberman's baffled! '*Where's my whimper?*' The cat's clearly confused! '*How come I've no meow?* The sound of their yawns had been silent to their keen ears until now. It's clearly audible and startles them! The anxiety the animals are exhibiting was expected. Yet, it's so cool to see it happen and brings smiles to the guardians and handlers. It's simply amazing! Dominic, one of the handlers, understands their confusion and feelings of fright! He walks over and kneels down between them. Looking first to the canine then to the feline he urges calmly, "Settle down, it's okay. Everything's okay. Trust me! You've been enhanced! All of you! Now we can really *talk*! You've always been able to communicate amongst yourselves and understand us! Now we can *truly* understand you!" The animals begin to chatter non-stop. They get them to calm after a while and Dominic addresses them:

"We need your help! What we're asking of you isn't without risk! But your help's badly needed because of your skills! We don't possess your abilities!" The canine Dominic had consoled makes his way thru the crowd of animals and positions himself directly in front of him. "I am Duke! *He turns his head to the feline.* Her name's Isisi! We'll do all we can!" He states in a grave reassuring bass voice. As Dominic looks about the room all of the animals heads are bowed to him in confirmation of Duke's words! "Thanks, Duke and thanks to all of you! Oh, yeah! Rule number one, 'Speak to and with none other than our species'. That'll be easy for all of you! You've the ability to detect us!" "That really wasn't necessary!" snaps Duke. Dominic grimaces. "For the next few weeks, together, we'll go thru intense training. We'll teach and learn from each other. Do any of you want to return to where you were?" A loud and resounding, "Hell no!" goes up from the unusual group. Still a few others can be heard emphatically avowing, "Hell to the No!" *This response causes hysterical laughter from the handlers and guardians!* Dominic raises his hands in mock surrender, "Okay! Okay! I get it! We get the message! And Duke I didn't intend any disrespect!" Duke looks to him, "No worries!"

CHAPTER SEVENTEEN
law enforcement revisiteo

10:00 a.m.
Philadelphia Police Headquarters
MAY 16TH

The detectives are seated inside an office on the second floor of the 'Round House' at Race Street. The F.I.B. agents aren't physically there, but via video conference! "Good-morning, Director Morrison! We've combed thru the records and the streets for more information on Smith and Wood. But there's just nothing there! They're more of a threat to themselves than the public! And except for the witnesses who saw the hooded guys, no one knows anything more! They left no prints or evidence of any kind to verify they were even at the scene. The bullets extracted from the victims and shells collected at the scene came from Twiddles gun. "Could this be a botched robbery? Wrong victims? Wrong address?" Deevers espouses. Johnson interjects, "Odd you should mention that thought! O'Mallee and I think that's exactly what happened! These people were just unfortunate victims!" "But then there's the question of the stinkin' substance? What is it? Where'd it come from?" O'Mallee queries. *The F.I.B. couldn't tell them that the substance had degraded and simply vanished before it could be tested as a matter of security. Instead they maintain a false narrative.* "We'll have to get back to you on that note! Our guys are still running tests." "No, problem! Listen! All of you have a good week-end while we can! Something about this entire situation just feels off! I can't explain it!" Deevers remarks. "We understand! It's rubbing us a little raw too! We're conducting investigations of all the businesses on Chestnut Street. We're going to keep digging. Maybe there's something going on that we're not aware of! You guys try to have a relaxing week-end!" bids Johnson before terminating the transmission.

activity review

MAY 12TH THRU 17TH

Their combined genius results in four different compositions of the 'Auton'. The research and development departments are able to utilize three of them to create products that resemble cooking oil, corn syrup and flour. These ingredients are key elements in the production of the food items they've chosen to use as the delivery system. For the children there'll be 'Sand Pebbles', fruit jellied candies. No child could or would resist them!

May 18th thru 20th

Semis world-wide are loaded with the reconstituted products to be delivered to the warehouses of distributors who supply baking companies, foreign and domestic, i.e. Bongarde, Bariolla, Entralux, Cara Lee, Delicious Cakes, Sweet Beam's, San Marcos and Hospitality Desserts etc. with these ingredients. When each reaches its targeted warehouse the current inventory's removed and replaced. In most cases the 'new' inventory's in usage within less than twenty-four hours. The trucks and drivers appeared routine causing no red flags!

May 24th

The *seedlings* receive the first shipment of freshly baked 'treated' goods and distribution world-wide begins. Delivery to those in the most remote places is first priority. Millions of PGG members manage tents at parks, varying events, softball, baseball, basketball, soccer, Little league games and fairs, distributing 'free' products. As projected the children easily gravitate to the 'Sand Pebbles.

May 29th

It's exactly five days since the introduction of the 'products' into the populous and striking results are already manifesting! Reports of criminal mischief by Tauri takes a marked plunge. No Tauri have been injured or died of senseless violence nor bullets of law officers. Teenagers and adults, young and old, have abandoned the degrading prison-style known as, 'sagging' and other forms of unbecoming dress. Now they desire design and structure accompanied with knowledge, elegance, dignity and grace! The disgraceful display and disgusting practice of tattoos has become passe! Parlors no longer enjoy a smorgasbord of ignorant, mindless clients! Drug traffickers and dealers are quickly vanishing from the landscape! A definitive change's occurring! Even their physical condition's affected! Tauri are no more afflicted with hypertension, gout, arthritis, diabetes, obesity, mental disorder, blindness, deafness, Lupus, leukemia, cancer etc. The therapy also affects the 'nebis', a region of the cerebella, thru the production of maiphens that stimulate the cells and cause them to regenerate and dissolve the protein barriers that've formed at the doorways of the KSCs.

Libraries are realizing 100% activity in every category from A to Z, by the young and the old. The turnaround time for every book's less than thirty-two hours! At this rate every book will be read in less than four months by every individual in the 'affected' areas. Change's becoming evident! Also once the auton's consumed the individual becomes habituated. Their future requirements will be distributed from the most unlikely places.

May 30th

Global markets are experiencing abrupt decreases in consumer spending across the board. Retail stores, food markets and corner stores are realizing a 65% reduction in sales and profits. Rumors of lay-offs and store closures hangs in the air! Local farmers and green merchants are experiencing a welcomed 110% increase in profits and traffic for vegetables, fruits and fresh meat! Natural gas companies and fuel suppliers are experiencing an 89% decrease in profits! They're (the corporations, conglomerates) victims of consumer bullets and hemorrhaging 'green blood'! How's this possible they rave pointing fingers blindly at each other! Meanwhile the beds of hospitals are filling with victims (BTs) suffering unexplainable life threatening conditions! On the other hand, Tauri (ATs) are vacating their beds due to healing! In time they'll realize the cause! As arrogant, ignorant and bigoted as the Bahleide/BTs are, it's going to take precious time for them to fully realize and accept what's happening! Time they no longer have!

May 31st

There's been an explosion of reported accounts on the news and countless U-Tube videos of innocent people of coloration by majority and a minority of 'light ones' being intimidated without justification by (BT) bigoted citizens and law officers drawing and firing their weapons without cause! The strangeness is that the discharged bullets do not impact their intended targets, but ricochet back to their source...the weapon of its origin and the shooter! After ninety-five thousand law enforcement deaths globally, twelve thousand civilian and sixty thousand police officers in North Americas alone! Law enforcement realizes it can no longer harass the innocent without consequence! For once they...FEAR!

Positive changes are manifesting around the world. Wars and conflicts are de-escalating rapidly. The only conflicts that exist are among BTs! The senses of the Tauri are developing. Soon they'll be able to detect each other thru voice frequency, smell, as well as being able to see auras. BTs have no auras and they smell badly! The Tauri are uniting on an unbelievable scale!

CHAPTER NINETEEN
confidencial updace

JUNE 2ND

*B*etween Jae's new responsibilities, catering business and law practice *(which is currently involved in litigation with a high profile conglomerate regarding corporate negligence) free time's been elusive. It's been three weeks and she's yet to speak with Doe in her capacity as 'confidante'.*

Its early evening when she impulsively pushes the button on her 'cd'. It rings for a moment then a soft, sultry French accentuated voice answers, "Hello!" "Good-evening, Commander! This is a S.O.L call! (sign of life) I'm checking on you!" *Doe's surprised to hear her voice, but elated and she chuckles!* "Oh! Jae! How good of you to call! Everything alright?" "All's well! This is our call, Commander. Sorry it's taken me so long! How're you?" *She smiles a smile that Jae cannot see!* "Oooh! You're serious! This is personal!" "Yes, ma'am! Now! Tell me what's riding you! I can hear it in your voice." "Okay, Jae! First please stop addressing me as commander and ma'am! Secondly, I'm alright!" "Uh…huh! Okay, Doe! And what else?" "Oh, my! Aren't we aggressive! Alright! If you must know, I'm disturbed by the environmental report released today! Jae! Forty years ago, Nate and I tried thru mediators to alert the scientific communities and corporations that carbon build-up had entered the red zone and that immediate actions, installation of infiltration systems and reversing from fossil fuels to solar and wind energy were imperative to arrest and prevent future build-up. However, our efforts were fruitless! They've exceeded the red zone! It really may be too late! Jae! They're suffocating *her*! She's slowly and painfully dying! They've no interest in abandoning their destructive methods! *Her voice saddens.* It's been and continues to be distressing and extremely frustrating having our hands tied, because we've always had the ability to alter the condition of the Tauri, who could in turn have help *Earth*! But we were bound by the Prime Directive, forbidden to interfere! We'd no choice other than to stand down. I confess! I worry for *her*! They've (BTs) defaced *her* so and the weight upon *her has become s-o-o* heavy! Jae, *she* gives them every-thing! The Bahleide and influential BTs world-wide are well aware of who *she* is! They don't care! Their level of arrogance, greed and selfishness is beyond decadent! But everything's changed now! Hopefully, we can still help *her*!" "Um…Doe, I really understand your feelings! How vicious and ignorant to dismantle and destroy the environmental regulations that Abamah put in place to protect *Earth* from further injury! It's justice to charge and demand those who've caused the damage (corporations) with the responsibility and expense of clean-up, prevention and restitution! They can pay for it out of their gouged, ill-gotten profits! It wouldn't cost the average Joe a dime! It'd be for the protection of *Earth* and generations, hopefully, to follow! But the stupid *average Joes* ignorantly side with those who could care less about them or *her*! They (corporations) laugh repeat-edly at their level of naivete and outright stupidity to rebel against their own interests! The *Joes* even dismissed the very people trying to alert them to help *Earth* and themselves i.e. Greenpeace, conservationists and envi-ronmentalists! The Tauri have been blinded to the reality of **their sacred duty** to safe-guard *her*! Must the air get so toxic it's un-breathable? Must it really become too late before they understand that the threats of the past and those of the present are real? Must more waters become poisonous and unsafe to drink? How many Flint, Michigans are yet to be revealed? Then there's the food supply. If they kill the insects what'll till the soil? How will the crops and flowers be pollinated? Must the soil become so contaminated by chemicals that nothing will grow before they believe? How much longer will people continue to voluntarily consume the tainted, unsafe boxed, canned foods and meat products processed under the worst sanitary con-ditions, following no regulations and containing chemical additives that become toxic to the body over time? It's as though it hasn't sank deep enough into their cerebrum that they're being poisoned! It's actually occurring! This society's a mess! It needs cleansing!" "Jae, calm yourself. There was a time when the view of the *Earth* from space was a green, brown and blue orb. She was radiant and the oxygen had a sweet fragrance! Now there's markedly less green because they've chopped down too many trees causing the oxygen levels to drastically fall! And that once sweet fragrance's long gone from the oxygen! The only surviving example of atmospheric fragrance is when it rains! The scent of rain! Certain areas of the oceans have lost their azure hue due to pollution resulting from numerous oil spills! Yet, everyone's blind to the devastation occurring daily everywhere, every second of the day across the globe! Jae, the world wasn't designed to be fueled via currency! It was meant to function purely on goodwill and love! The light BTs of North Americas and other BTs native to their lands have clearly demonstrated their lack of compassion over and over thru out time! They're heinous beings! They'll never change! They can't! That's why it was important for us to develop strong safe-guards (*mechanisms)* for the Tauri. *Mechanisms* for which Bahleide and BTs have no defense! Never again will they harm or rule over the Tauri or the feminine! Their protection's permanent! There will be matriarchal governance! No worries! All's going to be well!" "Doe, I hear and feel you! But what really gets to me is the ugly, grotesque, vile swine who took over from Abamah and occupies the 'People's House'! He's a despicable being! Every word that drips from his drooling, foul mouth's a lie! The '*thing's*' incapable of speaking truth! The 'ogre' claimed to be at the top of the class, but refuses to show his academic transcripts and his cohorts have hidden them away for fear they'd prove how dumb he really is! He even had others intimidate institutions he'd attended not to release any of his records! There couldn't be a clearer sign of his academic deficiency! His G.P.A. and SAT scores must have been so low his father had to pay for his diplomas! I wonder if he has ADHD or Alzheimer's? Yet, he had the audacity to challenge the eloquent, easy on the eyes, Abamah's academic achievements which showed every time he opened his mouth! Then there's his exclusion from the war! He's a textbook example of the word COWARD! He lied about imaginary bone spurs. There were others with actual bone spurs who would've enjoyed the luxury of escaping the circumstances of war! But they were brave patriots who loved their country! They were real men and responded to the call! More importantly the ogre's politically, socially and intellectually unfit for the seat of C.O.T.A. The feminine 'mule' candidate had her share of problems! But she was more than qualified to honorably execute the duties and office of the C.O.T.A. with expertise and proficiency! We now know she would've been a better choice! *Hindsights twenty-twenty! Gotta get it right next time!* The ogre lavishes praise upon ruthless despots, blood thirsty beings and stands by lily-livered and silent as citizens of North Americas and journalists are unduly detained in foreign lands, beaten, tortured, jailed and in some instances killed! He nullifies the security clearances of highly qualified seasoned intelligence personnel, but orders his sibling idiots and spouse both who lack *political* experience be given the same clearances. All the while the son's wife's poor financial situation is a compromising factor that could compel her or both to deliver secrets of North Americas and the world to foreign adversaries for their own profit! It's mind-blowing that forty percent of the populous of North Americas refuses to see the truth and the unfitness of the 'mad swine' due to their self-hatred! They're BTs. He shuts down the government for no bona fide reason, over an unnecessary wall, without regard of its consequences or the hardships it'll cause! The Russian, pulling his strings, calling all the shots, is a delusional despot! But he's living his dream of domination in his country and he's *brainwashed* the swine he can have the same in the Americas! After all, the Russian's 'KGB', a master manipulator! You know I'd like to put the 'mindless ogre' in a cage, along with his *spawns* and see how okay they'd be with that condition!" *Her use of the word 'cages' rekindles Doe's memory of Tah's message to her.* "Jae, I hear you! He gets to me too! His followers suffer from Munchausen syndrome! You must remember they're BTs!" "Doe, you've hit the nail on the head!" "Oh, Jae! Before I forget again, Tamesh sends a message. She says to tell you, 'Cages are a go!' But getting back to you. You must calm yourself. Everything's going to work out! All will be corrected!" Nate enters and she turns to him. "Doe, excuse me! But could you please come to my room for a minute?" She looks to him with kind eyes and an understanding smile, "Sure! Just give me a few seconds." He's baffled as he leaves the room! She'd been pleasant! Normally! She didn't like being interrupted! "Sorry, Jae. I've got to go, but thank-you for thinking of me! This has been good!" "No problem! Doe! Thanks for listening to me rant! You know? You can call me anytime!" "I don't mind listening to you rant! And I will call you! Be well, Jae!" *Doe ponders, 'How did Tamesh know about Jae and cages? Oh, that's right! The keepers have special insights!'*

She enters Nate's room with a smile on her face! "Who were you talking to?" he probes. "Oh, just a friend!" *He smirks with a nod of disbelief!* "Hmm…hmp! Yeah! Just a friend. Well! Whoever it is I hope they keep calling, because I like that smile!"

CHAPTER TWENTY
RETURN TO
locus angeli

JUNE 21ST

O n the day of their departure back in May they'd agreed to return to Locus Angeli on this day for check-ups and information updates. The Beals had other reasons for requesting their return. The first was to begin *Zeatus, a* secondary therapy, to introduce them to the *other seedlings,* lastly to witness the effect of their handiwork. Doe had begun dosing them with 'Zauton' on the eve of their initial meeting to jump start the process of cerebral and neural conversion. They're now primed for the initiation of the anatomical alterations.

*Update-

Since they were last together Claire and Jae have been juggling time between the mission, networking with organizations and their business concerns. Ko's continued to perform miraculous procedures and Hakeem's company has won another bid for the construction of another bridge!

They arrive late morning and Shane's their only welcome. After exchanging greetings Claire questions, "Do you know what our suite assignments are?" Baffled a bit he squints and cocks his head to the side, "Claire! Your suite hasn't gone anywhere! It's right where you left it. Did you not understand?" *Now she's puzzled.* "You mean?" He smiles, "Yes, Claire. The suite you were given is yours! It was refreshed and sealed the day you departed as were the others and unsealed only this morning!" "Hmp! Wow!" she comments. The others snicker, shake their heads, proceed up the steps, thru the door and look about. They don't hear any movement and there're no signs of Doe nor Nate. "Let's check the Mango Room." Hakeem suggests.

Mano's face lights up as they enter! "Welcome back! Welcome home! It's wonderful to see you!" "It's great to be back and thank-you!" they return as they share hugs, kisses, handshakes and man-hugs! "Where's Doe and Nate?" Ko inquires. "Oh! They're on the cabana!" "Okay! We'll be back!" Mano nods with a smile as they empty out the rear exit onto the white sand. "Good-afternoon!" They greet as they enter. Doe and Nate have risen to greet them. *They'd felt their spirits!* "My…My! All of you're a sight for sore eyes!" she quips smiling! After hugs and kisses Nate looks to her, "Umm… Doe! Aren't you're forgetting our guests!" The trio had noticed five sitting with their backs to them and assumed they were staff. At that moment, Angela, Ivory, Neemah, Laura and Grant turn to face them! Hakeem smiles and Angela rises to greet him! Ko's twice shocked! The first is Neemah and the second's Ivory! He rushes to them! Claire's as shocked to see Ivory as he is! Claire's twice as shocked by Lauren's presence! Now it all makes sense! Who knew? Grant's unfamiliar, but extremely friendly and handsome! They exchange introductions and greetings! Despite all the commotion Claire notices Doe's eyes are still trained on the doorway. She moves to her. "Doe! Jae's not with us."

Her eyes glint momentarily, "What do you mean? Has something happened?" Well…yes! She called me yesterday, early evening after receiving a distress call from one of her kids (*all young adult men/ women 15-17 years of age*). Seems the father's an alcoholic deadbeat with a history of abuse. I didn't hear anymore from her, so I assumed everything had gone well! I had every confidence we'd meet this morning. Now I don't know what to think! Should I call her?" "No. Do you know if Freddie was with her?" "Oh, yes! Without question! She covers her like a blanket!" Doe looks away.

Nate's been observing them. He glances down at the time and grimaces! He's not worried as much as he's concerned she hadn't call him! They'd spoken an average of four times a week and it wasn't always official business! But he stands silent! There's no indication of conflict or injury! They must wait! Doe moves to him and challenges, "Is there something Jae doesn't care for about me? I really thought we had good kinship!" Shocked by her question he shoots a darting glance and shakes his head with a brief chuckle, "Doe! Why would you think such a thing?" His eyes soften and he smiles, "No worries! Trust me! She's your biggest fan!"

Hakeem and Angela move toward the exit. Ko takes notice and hollers, "Hey Keem! Where ya headed?" Doe laughs looking to him, "Come on! He's your best friend! By now you know exactly where he's going!" He chuckles and shakes his head, "Oh yeah! Hungry right?" "Nothing but! Angela seriously! You must have him checked for worms!" *The room fills with laughter!* As the group meanders toward the exit Claire pauses and whispers, "How can we leave her alone? Surely, there's something outside the confines of Locus Angeli she'd enjoy!" The conversations create a 'humming sound' easily detected by her, "Is there a problem?" she challenges. "Yes, Commander, there is! We're deserting you!" She smiles lowering her head for a moment, "You honor me with your concern! But I am, for the moment, senior in command. It's my desire, my order, that all of you relax and enjoy this time because it's ever fleeting! I've matters to attend. I'm fine! But your concern's most noted and highly accepted!" Nate turns to her, "Are you sure?" She smiles and gives him the *look!* "You know I can't tolerate them! He nods resignation and joins the others.

After they've left she removes her footwear, walks out the ocean front exit and steps onto the soft, warm, white sand. Gentle trade-winds kiss her face as she walks along the shore and warm waters heave back and forth soothingly across her feet. She absorbs the beauty surrounding her and ponders, '*How regretful that the majority of the Tauri, past and present, never saw an eighth of Earth's spectacular places! Even more remorseful is the reality that too many will never know her beauty that exists around the world! A lifetime ago, the Honorable Marcus Garvey had an epiphany! To introduce the Tauri of the North Americas with those in the Southern Americas and Africa. In many instances they'd have discovered relatives! However, the vast majority were ill-educated and had been mentally programmed to be fearful of anyone that spoke against the BTs. Thus, they feared the very mention of revolting against them! The rope of bondage that the Bahleide and BTs had woven over the centuries thru generations, at that time, required a much sharper, stronger weapon to breech its integrity.'*

Her moment of contemplation's interrupted by the movement of a young boy squatting a few feet ahead at the water's edge. His parents sit further up on the beach observing him. She approaches them, "Good-afternoon, Marisol and Brian!" They're stunned she knows their names! They'd seen her on occasions, but only from a distance. Never had they been this close! At this moment what others had claimed about their encounters with full-blooded Almadians is confirmed! The heat of her spirit's causing them to sweat profusely! Doe's a beautiful statuesque creature, regally attired and a soft, sweet seductive fragrance engulfs her! "Good-afternoon! Commander!" they return. "Is that your son, Haji? Why's he so sad?" "Yes, sir! He lost his best friend, Lee, in the Cold Creek High school shooting last Friday." Doe lowers her eyes and exhales, "I see. I bid you good-day! Be well!" She bids walking away.

As she nears him he senses her presence, stands and turns to her. "Hi! Haji! I'm sorry for what seems to be a loss to you! But I cannot share in your sadness!" Haji frowns in confusion and his demeanor shifts, "No disrespect! But lady? Who a-r-e you?" Her eyes narrow and voice softens, "Your parents will explain about me. Haji, I'm here to assure you that Lee's not dead. The phase people call death is not the end, but the start of a new beginning! A process of evolution to a more advanced existence." She takes three steps forward, throws her arms up in surrender and invites, "Come! Pat me down. Please I insist!" He pauses a moment before honoring her request. She's clean as a whistle! "Haji! The D.O.O. doesn't waste life energy! The D.O.O. merely recycles." He squints with a frown, "What's the D.O.O.?" "The D.O.O. is short for *Divine Omnipotent One*! The D.O.O. is *All*!" "So? There're no gods?" "Correct! Arrogant males have strived to equate and portray themselves as the alternative embodiments of many mythical gods i.e. Thor, Odin, Buddha etc. They over-stepped their bound-aries many, many, many, many, centuries ago by attempting to represent the Divine. The *D.O.O.* isn't confined to some far off place or a humanoid shell! They're all around us! *Earth's* the embodiment of *their* handiwork! Haji! Trust me. Take my hand!" They clasp hands and kneel down on the sand. "Now stretch your arms out like this!" She demonstrates and he fol-lows her lead. Within seconds their hands are sucked into the sand. Their eyes shut involuntarily as *Earth* fills them with *her* spirit! The parents are in observance and baffled by their body movements! When their *commune* ends, they stand, their eyes open and they smile to each other. "I have a gift for you!" She reaches inside her cape-like garment and withdraws a small, ornate, gold birdcage containing a rare beautifully colored mynah and offers it to him. He stands transfixed for a moment before accepting it! *He'd patted her down and she'd had nothing on her! No hidden devices! Nothing!* She walks away. He holds up the cage and peers at the bird. Then he places it on the sand and opens the door. The bird flies out, settles on the sand and transforms into Lee, his deceased friend. He's well-groomed, immaculately attired and has a glow about him. "Hi Haji! Don't be afraid! Ska-boom-boom!" That expression had been their secret code word.

Hearing it settles him. "It's really me, Haji!" he assures offering his hand for their secret handshake. Haji's hand trembles and shakes like a leaf as he reaches out to clasp his hand! He's amazed to feel its warmth and flesh similar to his own! He's not a ghost! "How's this possible?" "You know how we always thought that death was the boogie man? Well, Lee! Turns out we were way wrong! And the *D.O.O.'s* real! *They* wanted you to see me, on this plane, one last time to prove to you there's nothing to fear! A part of me will remain with you in the form of this bird until you find peace within yourself! Then it'll return to me! You're going to be fine, my friend! I've got to go now." Tears flow steadily from Haji as he hugs him for the last time. "I'll miss you, Lee!" "I'll miss you more!" "Ska-boom-boom!" they repeat in unison as they release from their embrace. Lee transforms back into the beautiful bird and returns to the cage.

Haji's pep has returned to his steps, his tears are gone and his demeanor's changed dramatically as he approaches his parents carrying the cage. His mother questions, "Where'd that come from?" "The lady gave it to me!" he replies smiling. *They don't know what she said to him, nor where the cage or the bird came from! But his grief's lifted and he's back to himself! For them that's enough!* "The bird's beautiful! What's its name?" his father queries. Cheerfully he replies, "Lee!" Marisol and Brian look to each other speechless! "Mom? Dad? Who was that lady?"

The craft carrying Jae touches down at 2:49 p.m. Doe returns to her suite shortly before 3 p.m. quickly sheds her clothing and begins to refresh. Jae knocks on her door at 3:10 p.m. but there's no answer. She tries the knob. It's unlocked. She opens it part way, sticks her head in and calls out. Still there's no answer. As she nears the bathroom she hears activity! She returns to her suite, nudges her shoes off, tosses a few items onto the bed, steps out on the balcony and eases onto the chaise lounge. She exhales deeply, relaxes and absorbs the serenity of the view.

3:40 p.m.

Doe steps out of the vessel refreshed, dons her robe and walks out into the open space of the suite. She pauses, closes her eyes, inhales and smiles! She detects her scent! Once dressed and groomed she knocks on her door. But there's no answer! She tries the door knob, steps in and finds her bed undisturbed, but a few of her belongings scattered on it. She scrutinizes the space. While she can smell her, there's no Jae! As a last resort she checks the balcony. There she lies on the chaise sound asleep! Doe rests against the door frame, arms crossed, scanning her from head to toe with a smile! But the smile isn't friendly! It's something much more dangerous!

Nate and Claire had stayed behind to play chess while the others had gladly taken advantage of another chance to 'surf' with Michael! As expected the *surfers* return loud, laughing and totally wound-up! Doe, Claire and Nate hear their commotion and rush to assist them to their suites to sleep it off! After which Claire goes to Doe's suite and knocks.

"Come in!" Claire steps inside, "Sorry to bother you! Have you heard from Jae?" "No. But she's here! Have you checked her suite?" "No. I thought I'd check with you first." "But why? You have the ability to retrieve any information you require!" "Commander, forgive me! I haven't gotten use to all of this yet!" "No need for regret! Now go and check on her! Let me know she's well!"

Claire knocks lightly on Jae's door. Hearing no response she tries the doorknob and walks in. The sitting area's vacant and the bathroom too! But some of her stuff's on the bed. She walks out onto the balcony and sees her asleep on the chaise. She smiles, turns and exits. That's when it hits her! *'How did Doe know Jae was back?'*

6:30 p.m.

An explosion of party music fills the entirety of *Locus Angeli* initiated by Doe! This was rare! There'd only been smooth jazz and island rhythms played on the audio and that was only during business hours and she'd never programmed any of it!

There's a soft knock on Doe's door a little before 8 p.m. "Come in!" she invites fumbling with the last earring. Jae steps inside, "Good-evening! Doe! You look amazing! Oh! I hope I'm not interrupting!" *Doe's momentarily motionless and speechless by the sight of her! She's absolutely stunning! Quickly she gathers herself!* "Of course not! Welcome back and thank-you, Jae!" "I stopped by earlier, but you were indisposed and I didn't want to disturb you! Plus, I was oddly exhausted!" "Well? How're you feeling now? You appear well rested!" "Oh, I'm alright! I feel recharged! Are you interested in hearing my report of the past twenty hours?" "Yes, of course! But the others should also hear! We were all very concerned for you! I think the perfect moment would be during cocktails." "Yes!" "Good! Shall we join the others?" Jae gives a smiling nod. *Doe's curious to what her reaction will be when she sees the others.* Ivory, Neemah, Lauren, Angela and Grant are seated at the bar conversing with Mano as they enter, "Good-evening, everyone!" Doe greets cheerfully! As they turn to her voice Jae's eyes nearly pop out of her head and a smile spreads across her face. She leans to Doe's ear, "Now I understand. I've been guarded all my life, haven't I?" Doe smiles lowering her eyes, "Why of course!" Ivory and Lauren leave their seats and greet her warmly, "Come!" They return to the bar and introduce her to Neemah and Grant. Within minutes, Nate, Hakeem and Ko enter. "Hey, Dorothy! Good to see you've returned safely from Oz!" Nate chuckles! "Yeah! Where's Toto?" muses Hakeem. *Laughter fills the room!* "Come! Let's sit together!" Doe invites moving to the lounge area. The others follow. She looks to Jae, "Now would be a good time to tell us what occurred!" Jae takes a breath and begins...

"About a year ago, near the end of August, we'd completed the quarterly inventory and everyone had left. I was securing the warehouse and heard glass breaking. Alarmed I pressed 911 on my phone. I was distracted by commotion coming from the office so I turned around and went back toward the office. I saw a teenager rummaging around, probably looking for something of value as I neared. When he saw me he held the bat defensively in front of him. At that moment I advised him of two facts! First, that the police were on their way and secondly, he'd be needing them and the rescue squad if he didn't put it down! He was scared and truth be told I was shaken! Turned out it was the first time he'd ever attempted anything of this nature or ever placed himself in legal jeopardy! It was an act of desperation! After a few tense moments he told me his name, and that his father was a rolling stone with other children he didn't support. He said they'd not seen him in weeks and they were hungry. When the police finally arrived I told them a story of kids playing and accidentally breaking the window with a ball so that his life wouldn't be forever marred by a record of aggressive behavior. I gave him money to give to his mother and offered him a job after school doing odd jobs and on week-ends as a server. Turns out he was good at both! His mother was an excellent seamstress and had a flair for design so I employed her too! She's now in charge of design and production of the uniforms for my employees. All they'd needed was the opportunity to be self-sufficient. His grades improved, his mother's dignity and the family's pride was restored and they were no longer dependent upon the welfare system! Until Saturday it'd been a little over a year since they'd seen him!

When he called I could heard the fear and pain in his voice as he pleaded with me to come! So Freddie and I climbed into the van. I left a note for Lauren, who was out of the office at the time! Now I know why! Anyway, as we pulled up I noticed someone peeking thru the blinds. It was Navar! There were a few neighbors, some nosy and others concerned gathered on the sidewalk. A few had come out onto their porches after hearing the ruckus created by the father. We exited the vehicle and walked up to his door. Before we could knock he opened it quickly and hurried us inside! He was shaking like a leaf, sweating profusely, bruised, bleeding, his lip was swollen and his shirt torn! At that moment, I felt like tearing the asshole apart!" "I didn't hurt him! I didn't touch him! I swear!" he repeated hysterically! "We continued toward the cries and moans of his mother and siblings coming from further inside the home as we urged him to calm down and recount what'd happened! He calmed somewhat and told us that his father had showed up about half an hour earlier. Of course he was drunk! He'd noticed their new furnishings and that his brother and sister were wearing new sneakers and riding bicycles. *The children had been outside riding when they saw him and rode back to the house as fast as they could to warn of his arrival and take their bikes in the house!* He'd forced his way thru the front door breaking the locks and started demanding money! Navar said he grabbed him by the throat and slammed him up against the wall. That's when his mother attempted to come to his aid! But he pushed her to the floor! He said it was at that moment that something strange happened! Instead of his intended kick landing to his mother the man was propelled backwards thru the air across the room! His body slammed against the wall with such great force it created a big hole! He said he tried to shake it off, stood up and charged them again! That's when his head turned violently as if an invisible left-upper cut had impacted his chin and lifted him off his feet! This time when he landed he didn't get up! He feared him dead and called me for help. Halfway there I placed an anonymous call to 911. The police were more than familiar with the man's history of abuse! We arrived fifteen minutes before them. When they arrived we identified ourselves as representatives from 'Earth Haven' and assured them we'd care for the needs of the family. They proceeded into the home to find the father in the corner writhing in pain and Navar's brother and sister huddled about the mother sitting in a chair in shock! After examining the man the paramedics discovered he'd four broken ribs, a jaw, right leg, a busted spleen and a concussion. They couldn't even cuff the monster to the gurney due to his injuries! Navar nor his mother's fingerprints or DNA was on the bum and they were free of his blood!" *His family had been the first Jae'd offered the therapy.*

The room's silent! Claire looks to Doe, "WOW! I'm liking this! The plan's really working! It sounds as if there were meta-physical ninjas within them!" Doe sneers, "Yes! It'll only intensify! However, there'll be situations like this where parent/s, relative/s or children will be of the opposite trait and rejected! They'll be outcasts! Whenever, wherever necessary we'll recover them and deliver them to sanctuaries that're being established and absorb them into *our bonah*! That's why the expansion of the networks and rehabilitation of acquired structures and properties is so important!" Hakeem clears his throat. Doe gives him a quick glance! "Angela! Darn! You've got to have him checked! What kind of worm does he have?" *The roar of laughter fills the room!*

They dine in silence each calculating various outcomes of the distribution, giving every consideration of anticipated reactions, envisioning all possible scenarios of the therapy's affect and what more they could do to re-configure protection for Tauri. But one fact was certain! Never again would *Earth, her children* nor the *feminine* be oppressed! NEVER!

After the main course they move to the lounge and are surprised by the variety of desserts creatively displayed there! Petit Fours, Coconut cake, Strawberry Shortcake, Tiramisu, Red Velvet cake, Butter Pound cake,

German Chocolate cake, Sweet Potato Pie, Dutch Apple Pie, and Lemon Meringue. "This is a gift from the chefs! They aim to spoil you!" Mano offers smiling! "Mano! You're kidding? Right? This is for a party or something?" Grant queries. "Oh no! Grant! Why would you think I was uh? How do they say? Pulling a leg?" he challenges. "No! No! This is great! It's just…since Jae told us about her young friend's father, I feel like celebrating and the desserts would be perfect!" "Yeah me too! The dog got what he and others like him deserve! Betcha he won't touch another feminine!" says Ivory with glee! "Ya! Got that right! Especially after being all jacked up! It'll be at least six months before he can stand with support!" Jae snickers. *They erupt into laughter!* Ivory announces, "Yes, let's celebrate 'Change'!" "Girl, I'm so with you! Neemah quips. Grant please crank-up the music!" "Sure thing!" Each prepares a plate laden with many of their favorite desserts as they lounge and listen or dance to the music. Nate sits across from Hakeem who's apparently lost in thought. *Nate could've read his mind, but he didn't and he wouldn't unless it were a matter of life. "Earth* to Hakeem! Over." he calls out. He gives Nate a respectful glance and begins to rant, "Tauri of the world have been and continue to be exhausted with life under BT rule. It's especially true here in the North Americas! A place stolen thru thievery and blood-shed! Despite their conduct and murderous acts they've not and will never admit to their atrocious crimes and return what they've stolen! Instead they continue a constant campaign of denial and deny knowledge to all, but the BT few!

Their control over the Tauri of the North Americas and around the world's wrong! Their deceit's appalling! They continually force feed their images of false superiority every day, all day thru televised and printed advertisements, video programming and other avenues. People around the world demonstrated clear adoration for Abamah! The signs of spiritual and intellectual evolution were evidenced thru his election to the most powerful position on *Earth!* The Tauri, *her children* (light and colorful) of North Americas made it happen! They'd stood as one for the fourth time in history! His candidacy and eventual election also evidenced the vastness of the unified vote! For the first time, in a long time, there was enthusiasm, a feeling of agape love and unity! It was the first time they'd not only felt, but saw the power of their votes! The power their *mule* leaders had always assured them existed, within each of them and had helped cultivate! They'd supported a decent, intelligent, articulate man of unquestionable moral character, a faithful husband, a loving father and a man of public service who'd served others! Plus, he was very easy on the oculi! For all the right reasons and qualifications, finally a leader, the first of coloration, had come to alter life for *Earth* and *her children*.

The Bahleide feared the unity of strength that was evident and growing amongst the Tauri! They feared their loss of power! But more importantly they feared the Tauri might finally have learned the truth and were spreading it! That fear drove the 'light' BT elephants and the 'ogre' to conspire with the Russian fiend to interfere and cause chaos amongst the citizens and vigorously attempt to rig the outcome of the North Americas election. *The fiend is already active in Europe!* They too must be vigilant in their protests and unyielding in their defense against him and those like-minded! The BTs spread lies and attempted to sway judgement because they feared the growing Tauri voting power and their feminine candidate! Who was the superior! With her combined knowledge and experience she was more than up to the task! The communist fiend feared her most and still fears other feminine to follow! The Tauri will elect feminine governance going forward for two reasons; first for two hundred years there's only been men and it's barely been sufficient! Now it's time for the feminine to be C.O.T.A. and Vice C.O.T.A. They'll be experienced feminine Tauri, both committed to the whole. The feminine have always been more cohesive than males! It's the 'hallmark' of their governance! They're the ones who truly know how to cleanse the swamp the males have created. Secondly, to return the Americas back on track with *her* allies and begin the healing!" *All in the room are silent!* Hakeem's beyond upset and more than a bit furious! Doe gives him a serious look, "Whew! You've a lot of discontentment and rightly so! But you've no more need to worry! You understand that right? *He nods smiling!*

Conditions are being corrected! They'll be in good order well before we leave! Now let's celebrate our first evidence of success! Okay?" *He lowers his eyes briefly and gives a nod.*

The celebration comes to an end sometime after 9 p.m. They agree to meet in the café at 10 a.m. and bid each other good-night. Doe's first to head to her suite. After she's left their presence Nate invites the others to the cabana, except Jae. He gives her a special assignment.

Doe's changed into her nightwear and is about to engage her 'communication console' when it self-activates! Within seconds Tamesh appears wearing a kind smile! "How're you my dear? You look lovely! Having company?" "O-o-h no, Tah! My mind's full with thought, ideas of strategy and realities, but my soul's filled with a feeling, albeit warm, it's heavy!" she confesses seating herself. "Oh, my sweet one! You don't recognize it anymore do you? Poor dear!" *She's clearly baffled!* "Tah? Of what do you speak?" "I speak of love!" "Love? With who? With what?" "With your *one*! That's who!" "Yeah? And who might that be?" she challenges with heavy sarcasm. Frustrated by her feigning ignorance Tamesh returns, "Your '*one*' is among the grouping! I know you feel it! Because we feel it! We don't know which of them it is at this moment! But we know it's one of them! So, you can dispense with your show!" "That can't be right!" she protests sharply! Tamesh softens her tone, "Calm down. Calm yourself. You're Almadian and they're too! You'll figure it out! However, I must inform that since you've made contact with the spirit of your '*one*' your sexual composites that've laid dormant for s-o-o-o long have been awakened. You've got! Hmp…I'm unsure! But best estimate…seven or eight months to execute the 'joining' or you'll literally 'die' from lack of love! In your case, it'll be stubbornness to recognize and accept it! You really need to relax! Doe, all will be well! Uh…you might want to answer your door!" She suggests as her image fades! Doe rolls her eyes, exhales and lays her head back against the chair. *She'd not heard any noise before nor does she hear any now!*

Within five seconds there's a soft knock on her door! She opens her oculi, rises and answers it. She's surprised to see Jae holding a small box. "Uuh.....uh...excuse my intrusion, but Nate asked me to give this to you. I'm so sorry to bother you!" she stutters while offering the box. "Oh! Merci! Cherie, won't you come in?" *Jae's oculi quickly roam about the room.* "Don't you have company?" *Perplexion crosses Doe's face.* "No! Why would you think that?" "Because you're dressed so--!" *She chuckles with a slight shake of her head.* "Jae, this is just nightwear...pajamas! Come in." Jae steps inside. Doe takes the box, sets it on the bar then moves to the lounge area, takes the few steps down into the 'pit and curls into a corner of the sofa. Jae follows, curls into the opposite corner and eyes her. "What's bothering you?" "I didn't say anything was bothering me!" "You didn't have to! Look! I know we've not spent much physical time together. But we've talked a lot! I've learned to understand your voice and your demeanor." "Well, aren't you special?" Jae gives her a *look.* Doe exhales and casts a long stare to her, "Please! Forgive me!" "No worries! What's wrong?" "Oh! I just get...what's the word? Ahh...frustrated because Bahleide are well aware of the Tauri's superiority! They've plotted against us since the 'Great Upheaval and theft of the 'Compendium'!" Jae cocks her head contemplatively, "That's the third time I've heard mention of the 'Great Upheaval'. Just what was it? What happened?" A glow grows about Doe's face and her eyes return to Jae, "There was a time when the world exercised a communal system of governance guided by a feminine council comprised of queens representing tribes across the globe prior to the 'Upheaval'. From every region a feminine was selected by their tribe to be representative of the whole. These representatives formed the world council and selected the wisest from amongst them to be...the 'GQ', guiding queen!

Their governance was family-like in its structure; planning and taking care of the whole! The highest consideration and regard for *Earth* was first and foremost! They easily communicated with *her* and each other because there were no breaches and land travel was unrestricted! The world was at peace! Then BT males from the northern regions (places of Bahleide *seeding)* of Europe ventured into Africa. The Tauri greeted these foreign-ers with open arms. They were intrigued by their strange appearance, but the foreigners were more mesmerized by them! After seeing how the dark and colorful ones lived, their governance, knowledge, educational struc-tures, pageantry and riches they set out to deceive and steal all they could before setting their armies upon them to slaughter. *She exhales.* All adult males/princesses and queens were killed first. They spared the educated that would cooperate to give them knowledge, but killed those who pro-tested and refused. In honor and protest of those killed the remaining edu-cated feigned cooperation and fed them partial knowledge and equations. In doing this they ensured that BTs would never have the true details of any knowledge and would lack the final step of all formulations and equa-tions! That's why craft fall from the sky, airbags kill, robotic driven vehicles malfunction and the hover board toy explodes and catches fire! The chil-dren spared were used as personal slaves and objects of sexual abuse." Jae interrupts, "So, I'm guessing that the proof of feminine superiority, jour-nals, annals and other records were also destroyed!" *Doe looks to her with a sneer.* "Yes, but there is a record! It's hidden with the 'Compendium.'" Jae nods, "That explains why they're always collecting our artifacts of history as well as others of coloration and claiming them for their own! They've taken credit for so much stolen knowledge, because they had little of their own! They falsely portray themselves as the masters and work hard at that deception! That's what made Ivory get involved in the study of archaeol-ogy. She said she'd always felt that the feminine was the dominant and that the purpose of males was that of support. Heck! The majority of them are useless for anything more! Anyway she said her suspicions were confirmed on a dig in Turkey when she stumbled across what she and everybody else assumed was a rock jutting out of the ground. But her foot knocked off a large chunk of dirt revealing hieroglyphics. Ten months later an eight foot ivory bust of a black feminine of royal stature was raised. Her facial fea-tures were in perfect condition!" "I recall that unearthing! She's was and is beautiful!" Doe remarks reflectively! "Intentionally they discourage people of coloration from the study of archaeology for that reason! Plus, they're afraid that when the Tauri regain power they'll treat them as they've been treated!" "Very good, Jae! You get a gold star!" *Jae rolls her eyes feigning upset. Doe smirks.* "Can I fix you a 'Lotus'?" "Why thank-you! I thought you'd never ask!" Doe gives a piercing glance and moves to the bar.

Back in the cabana…

Nate's last to enter holding a small crystal bowl. He finds the group seated and in an involuntary state of deep contemplation! He takes the seat next to Claire and waits. The silence's so deafening it lends resonance to the sounds of the surf! Fifteen minutes have passed since he'd found them in this state! He scans the group and is about to check his watch once more when they suddenly return to awareness. Unaware they've experienced a lapse in time! Nate doesn't make comment. Instead he offers each a pink liquid capsule from the bowl. After each has taken one he informs, "This is your secondary therapy, the 'Zeatus'. It's the booster to further prepare your bodies for anatomical transformation. There'll be no pain and changes will not visibly manifest until you take the third and final therapy. We'll be checking regularly on your progress." He takes special notice of Hakeem's disapproving expression! "Hakeem! What is it? What's bothering you?" Hakeem gives a glance as he reclines in the chair, "Oh! It's nothing to do with us! You know! I was just thinking! As children we'd play cowboys and Indians. Blindly we always cheered for the 'light' BT cowboys! There were no Tauri of coloration on TV in those days! It took some time before we understood they were the murdering invaders and thieves who'd stolen North Americas from the Indians! None of them were the best nor the brightest! Quite the contrary! As a matter of fact many were misfits and outcasts! How stupid we were!" "I understand your feeling, Hakeem! But don't beat up on yourself! You were a child! But rest assured all's about to be corrected! Soon every Tauri, regardless of age or gender will be protected! And let's not be remiss! The majority of the 'light' are our 'bonah'! They're just unaware. Throughout history it's them who've protected, the colorful, Tauri from extinction! Despite them falsely identifying as 'BTs' they'll

144

awaken and be changed! We don't know what hue they'll be changed to, that's the authority of the D.O.O.! But two factors are certain! In short order they'll have coloration and we must save them!" "You'd think the so-called geniuses of the world would've figured out by now what the real problem is! Complete domination of North Americas by the light BTs!" "Oh, they're well aware! They know they've no right to be here! But they don't care! They lack souls and bask in chaos! It's all they know and desire! BTs are too vile to grasp the reality of their fate, but the Bahleide are well aware of it! North Americas and the world will never know peace until both are gone from *Earth!*" states Neemah. Claire interjects, "I agree! They've always pointed fingers at the colorful and castigated them to be the evil. While it's those among them who're executing the most heinous crimes. Tauri kids aren't the ones shooting up schools, mosques, synagogues or planting bombs!" "Nate? How long will the distribution of our 'products' remain in circulation? And what's our targeted goal?" questions Ko. *Nate smiles briefly.* "I was wondering which of you was going to ask! I should've known it'd be you! The initial supply of products covers a distribution period of thirty days. We'll monitor progression of affect daily. Within eight weeks we'll have a clear picture of just how many have been affected. At that point we'll plan further. Plus the other two *events* are in progress!" *His eyes shift to Claire.* "Now if you'll excuse me!" All eyes are on him as he offers Claire his hand. She accepts and they exit. The others pair off too!

Back in Doe's suite…

She pours two glasses half full and gently pushes Jae's to her. She sips. "Well?" "Hmm, Doe! This is s-o-o good!" *Doe sips her own.* "Yes! I must agree!" "Come! Let's sit out for a bit! I love the night!" Jae implores heading to the balcony. They sit quietly absorbing *her* moonbeams and observing *her* ocean waves. Below them a few walk along the shore, others are seated on the beach. They move to the railing to gain a better view. Timidly Jae inquires, "Doe? The Tauri are being weaponized aren't they?" Doe casts a stern glance to her. "Yes! Of course! I thought you understood that was the intention!" "Well, I did somewhat! But it wasn't until witnessing what happened to Navar's father that I realized the power! The therapy really does render them untouchable!" "Jae, soon the feminine will regain their power! Within a month or two they'll standardize a process of 'neutralization'…a true and thorough recycling process and formulate applications to apply to the air, land and the sea! In approximately a year and a half they'll have effectively and safely disassembled all oil rigs, refineries and nuclear facilities building materials, as well as, the toxic by-products they've produced. Junkyards will become an unpleasant memory of dysfunction. Please understand their weaponry's necessary to protect them against both Bahleide and BT aggression!" *Jae takes another sip.* "This society's a mess! It needs to be purged!" *Doe looks away from her to the stars.* "The Bahleide and BTs of North Americas and other regions of the world have demonstrated their absence of compassion, fairness and mercy over and over again thru out the annals of time via their callous acts and practices against *Earth* and others different from themselves! They've a long history of forced slavery, imprisonment, torture and terrorism! They'll never change! They can't! It's what they are! But from this day forth there will be a strong guard against them! Never again will they disrespect the feminine! We've laid the ground work for generational protection from now until long after we've gone and beyond. There's no need for concern!" "But Doe! To turn a blind eye to Flint, Michigan, Florida, Texas and the people of the storm ravaged island of Puerto Rico's disgusting and wrong! As far as the flag's concerned, none of the colorful need feel an ounce of reverence for it, nor should they! It was created for and made by 'light' BTs! The colorful weren't even treated with dignity, respected or even considered equal! Yet they still aided them in their wars and conflicts!" Jae pontificates. *Doe's eyes narrow, but her expression softens.* She moves closer to Jae, peers into her eyes and lays her hand gently on her arm. "They'll be fine! Trust! All will be well! Never again will the Tauri be exploited or oppressed!" In a tone of absolute command she emphasizes, "You must understand, Commander! Only on *Earth* has this catastrophic circumstance (male rule) occurred! It will be corrected. Never to happen again! The feminine have always been and remain dominant thru out the universe! Galactic or star wars are Bahleide propaganda, another lie promoted by the BTs via the Bahleide. Everything will be well here!" Jae nods, takes a deep breath of ocean air and returns her eyes to the sky. "*She's beautiful isn't she?*" Doe glances to her with a smile, "Yes, *she* is and so are you! You know? You're a wonderful group and others gravitate effortlessly to you!" Jae softens her voice and turns her eyes to her, "Excuse me! Were you suggesting I was avoiding you earlier?" "I can't lie, Jae. It crossed my thoughts!" She smiles coyly, "Doe, you're command! You've much on your mind, I'm sure! Plus! Even you must be somewhat shell-shocked by us and the new reality! I know we were and are! You can't convince me otherwise!" "You, my dear, are very insightful! It's of great comfort to have you as my confidante!" *Jae looks to her with a smile!* "Uhh…! Can I make a request of you?" "Why of course, anything!" "Will you fix me one more night-cap?" *Doe smiles.* "I'd be my pleasure! Come on, let's go in."

Jae swivels on the bar stool as Doe mixes and notices the beautiful canopy that conceals her bed. "That's a most exquisite canopy. It's beautiful! Do you mind if I take a closer look?" "No! Be my guest!" She rises, moves to it and runs her hand against the smoothness of the delicately woven silk fabric. Gently she pushes a portion of the panel back to reveal the oddly-shaped bed. Curious whether the bedding's soft, firm or hard she lays on it. It begins to recede downward into the floor! "Doe!" she cries out panicked! Doe chuckles for a moment before snatching the box off the bar and moving to the bed! *Jae's shaken!* "Oh, I'm sorry! I never had a reason to mention its features to you!" Doe offers between snickers! Jae gives her a *look*! "Well! Would you please help me up?" "No!" Doe taunts before pushing a button on the edge of its molding. The bed rises and locks in place. Jae jumps up as if stung by a bee! "Well, played Commander!" she retorts! Doe smirks as she hands her the box. "This is for you! It's Zeatus." Jae looks to her, "This is it! The true change?" "Another part of it, yes! Take it before you go to sleep." Right then and there she opens the box, withdraws the pink capsule and pops it into her mouth. Her action startles Doe! "You didn't have to do that!" she protests! "I know! But who better to share my greatest moment with than you?" *Doe drops her eyes trying to hide her blush!* "You're taking lessons in flattery from Hakeem aren't you?" *They laugh!* "Thank-you for our time tonight, Doe! But I insist you get some rest! See you in the morning!" she bids moving to the door. "No Jae! Thank-you! You're really good medicine!" "Good-night, Doe! Be well!" "Good-night, mon Cherie!"

CHAPTER TWENTY-ONE
activity review

During the second week of June five thousand sentinels are dispatched from the 'Plantation' to designated '*clusterhubs*' nationally and world-wide. Each carries an over-sized, titanium-type case containing five hundred *zeltrons*. Their targets are firearms and ammunitions manufacturing plants, independent, company storage facilities and warehouses and all casinos (foreign and domestic). They've seven days to complete their mission (planting zeltrons) and return to the '*hubs*' to await further orders.

June 19th

Around the world men from all walks of life, ethnicities, races, religions and status begin complaining and reporting stomach pain, pelvic area cramping and seek medical attention.

June 20th

Across the globe PGG members, male/female, roam the streets of major cities, townships, hamlets, provinces and little towns wearing black retro G-Men sunglasses. Their targets, 'sagging' pants. The sunglasses appear ordinary, but are weaponized and controlled by mind/eye coordination. The members simply meander thru crowded streets, market squares and malls searching for 'sagging' on display. *When detected, they focus on the targeted area.* Two beams (*invisible to the humanoid oculi*) expel from the corners of the glasses frames and 'tags' the area. It takes less than two seconds! The member moves on in search of a new target. This action's exercised from dawn to dusk for two days. After nightfall on the second and last day of this mission, June 22nd, the glasses are collected and returned to the '*hubs*'.

CHAPTER TWENTY-TWO
weeding the garden

Phase One - Step 1#

The 'Plantation's' located off the coast of Florida, on an island a bit smaller than the state of Delaware, in North Americas, inside the Bermuda Triangle. It's the home of one of two Almadian bases intentionally constructed centuries ago. This particular facility's for training purposes. It's abuzz with activity as SMVs and Whispers prepare for launch. Sentinels are busy loading pallets filled with 'GEBIs'. Each is programmed to detect, seek out and attack BTs. It will not self-destruct until all of its venom's been expended. The mission deploys at 2300 EST. The continent of Africa's the first target of attack for the obvious reason, it's sacred Tauri ground. The place where the colorful and light BTs committed unspeakable atrocities of stolen innocence and treasures of the land for far too long and lied about *her* history! Due to their brutal treatment of Africa they're first to feel the revenge of the fallen and wrath of the murdered unborn! Time to pay the piper!

Upon their arrival to the continent and *designated locations* Nouakchott, Nouadibou, Chegga, Bir Moghrein, Qualata and Selibabi, at 0600 hours they unload and begin setting up temporary camps. Others are busy opening boxes of 'GEBIs', removing the ice cube like trays they're packed in and setting them on the ground in rows of ten. The codes of the control devices for each lot are retrieved and fed into the main administrator. Within minutes of activation they ascend and fly off in search of targets!

The attack of the GEBIs spreads along the west coast of Africa and expands into the interior like a wildfire with the wind at its back! The kills are merciful, painless and clean...no blood, no bones! The chemicals within the venom causes the light of the sun to affect the dead bodies in the manner of 'Hollywood vampires! Only this is real! In the absence of sunlight the process of disintegration takes a couple of hours longer! The sentinels continue across the continent recruiting Tauri of age to train as sentinels along the route. Tauri have been starved of essential nourishment, clean, fresh water and medical attention far too long! They're fed 'therapy' saturated food and fresh, clean water. Once their hunger abates and thirst has been satisfied they sleep. While they're in slumber their KSCs begin opening. When they awake they're hungry for knowledge, truth and self-discovery!

New unfamiliar structures (housing) are erected. They're free of the undesirable conditions of shanties! The older feminine instinctively care for the orphaned and victimized (*genital mutilated and sexual assaulted*) children and young adults and form foster family units. Many of the newly liberated men, young and old are urged to remain as support to and for the feminine and to assist them with transitioning into their new life condition.

CHAPTER TWENTY-THREE
First Event Reaction

JUNE 23RD

6:00 a.m. (*time zone specific*) the victims of 'tagging' are awakened by the discomfort of irritation and a burning sensation across the buttocks. The sensation intensifies every hour generating extreme pain and heat until third degree burns manifest on BT victims and first degree on a few hundred Tauri caught off-guard! The majority of Tauri are self-respecting and wear their clothing decently which accounts for fewer victims. The third degree injuries are disgusting, horrible sights! Attending doctors, nurses and aides are enthralled by the mysterious phenomenon!

6:45 a.m. From the board rooms to the streets, BT males around the world from all walks of life and ethnicities are sharing pain and discomfort! They've been complaining of discomfort for days. They've never felt anything like this and do not understand the aching, itching and cramping sensations they're experiencing in their pelvic area!

7:00 a.m. EST- The unattractive, fugly, press secretary of the 'mad ogre' makes an astonishing announcement. She reports that all the *elephant* congressional and senatorial members have been stricken with the chicken pox! Once again they lie to the public to conceal the truth!

8:25 a.m. EST- Washington D.C. – Between 6:00-6:59 a.m. the *elephant* congressional and senatorial bodies were affected including the egotistical, lying, lunatic ogre and the lying new 'court' man! It's safe to assume they'll be no more 'grabbing by the pussy' nor mention of it! Now they're the bitches! The *Mules* are unaffected!

10:30 a.m. JPT- Sora Kagome, CEO of Hiroko Industries, an electronic conglomerate, sits in his chair at the head of the conference table in the boardroom. As he speaks he's overcome by severe cramping in the pelvic area. The others abandon their chairs and rush to his aid. One pulls out his phone and calls for help. The EMTs show-up, take his vitals, load him onto the stretcher, strap an oxygen mask to his face and hurry from the room. It isn't until the EMTs had gone and the commotion died down that they notice how much blood stains the chair where he'd sat!

10:40 a.m. EST- Inside the KKUL network's boardroom, at New York's Rockefeller Center, its president, Steve Wilkerson's on a conference call when he's suddenly overcome by severe cramping. He's unable to complete the call and his assistant steps in!

Most of the victims reach a medical center within an hour or so! Every physician's baffled by what they see! How could? How did this happen? What's causing this? Needless to say, some of the 'organ reassignment' casualties literally lose their minds upon being informed their condition's permanent and fall victim to suicide! Others suffer mental break-downs, heart attacks, drug overdoses and others demand a cure!'

Later that morning,

Others are in the midst of oral presentations or video conferences, digging ditches, operating heavy equipment or sitting at desks when the blood begins to run down their legs without warning! *The only variable's the time of occurrence due to time zones.* Of course they panic and seek the nearest medical facility. Upon physical examinations startling discoveries are made! Testicles have shrank to the size of a grain of rice and there's no penis! Instead a hairy, bleeding vagina fills the space! They're experiencing menstrual periods and they've ovaries! Now they'll know what the feminine go thru! Its poetic justice for the feminine of the world! Males will now have cause to consider and reflect on a host of feminine related issues!

The tirades of the maniacal C.O.T.A are markedly mute this morning for the first time in twenty-three months! The press finally has something more important to cover other than his insane tweets, inflammatory and insulting ravings and pre-arranged photo-ops! He's been upstaged by bizarre events and the deaths of law enforcement officers. Plus, he's a new personal concern that even his physician cannot cure! He whines as a frustrated child with a fully loaded diaper because he's uncomfortable with his new bleeding vagina! Towards noon his deafening profane orations and nonsensical rantings echo thru-out the East wing! He's so deficient of intelligence he's unable to grasp the gravity of what's occurring!

By noon around the world, eyewitness accounts of strange phenomenon dominates the media. Reports of elderly residents of nursing facilities being restored to vitality are pouring in! News of the sex re-assignments has 'blown-up' the media! The true number of victims won't be known for three weeks.

CHAPTER TWENTY-FOUR
second event

JUNE 23RD
8:30 a.m. PST

For the residents of Hacienda Heights it's a comfortable eighty degrees and a soft breeze tickles the leaves of palm trees. It's a beautiful day and Benjamin Ruizzo's birthday. He's sitting in his living room sipping coffee and watching the early morning news when the phone rings. As it rings for the third time he reaches over and answers, "Hello?" "Happy birthday! Son!" returns a cheerful female voice that rings familiar! He pauses! It can't be! But it sure sounds like her! "Mom?" he challenges in a voice filled with confusion and disbelief! She chuckles, "Yes, Benjisan, it's me! Your mother, boy! I'm so glad to have this chance to wish you a happy birthday! I've missed so many! *She offers sorrowfully.* You've been a loving and faithful son! Always making certain I was well taken care of! I want you to know how grateful I am to and for you! But now it's time for you to get on with your life! No more worrying for me! Please son! Go on with Monica and be happy! She's a keeper, Benjisan! I'm so very proud of the man you've become and your father is too! We love you so very much and you'll always be in our hearts!" After listening for a few seconds, he realizes it really is his mother! By her voice, to the way she called him, Benjisan. *She's the only one to ever call him by that name!* "Mom, where are you?" "I'm with friends! I have to go now, but remember what I've told you! Happy birthday! We love you very much! You're in our hearts forever!" The phone goes dead. On his caller id there're no digits. Just the word 'unknown'. A startled look comes over his face! It was her voice! Despite it having been years since he heard it! His father died in the Vietnam war and his mother's been a long time resident at the 'White Dove'. An upscale, state of the art, long term nursing facility. She'd suffered a stroke eleven years ago and it'd left her paralyzed from the waist down. To add insult to injury, less than a year later, she was diagnosed with a severe form of Alzheimer's. For the past four years she hadn't recognized him and he'd not heard her voice until now. But the voice on the phone was her! It was mom! She sounded like her happy self! But how did she know about Monica? She's never met her! And what friends is she referring to? Ben picks up the phone and dials the 'White Dove'.

The line's busy on the first effort, but not the second. "Good morning, White Dove! How may I direct your call?" offers the somewhat chirpy voice. "My name is Ben Ruizzo. My mother is a resident. I need to speak with her attending nurse!" he demands.

The receptionist recognizes the name, as one of the sixty-five, on the list of those missing! She beckons for Allison Webster, the head administrator of the facility to her station. Allison moves to her quickly and bends to hear her whisper, "I have Mr. Ruizzo. His mother's on the list" Allison takes a few calming, deep breaths. She's spoken only a few times with him concerning his mother's care. He'd been a reasonable, civil, pleasant guy! But now he'd every reason to be the opposite! "Mr. Ruizzo, we have a situation…." Before she can utter another word he hangs up, grabs his keys, jacket and heads out to his car. Traffic is light. The ride to the 'White Dove's a bit faster!

As he pulls into the parking lot there're local police and F.I.B. agents (his co-workers) crawling all over. His sometimes partner, James Eaton notices him, "What're you doing here?" "What's going on?" Ben challenges. "Uh, some of the residents are missing!" "What the hell do you mean missing?" Before Eaton can respond another agent standing in the entrance beckons them. As they approach he informs, "The facility's ready to run the surveillance footage." Along with the others (local police and F.I.B. agents) Ben gathers around the monitors. At first there's nothing unusual as personnel check-in and out of their shifts. Then six minutes into the footage according to the time stamp 12:06 a.m. a group of maybe fifty or sixty people are walking, talking excitedly and laughing as they travel down the corridor towards the exit doors. They're well-groomed and dressed impeccably elegant evening style. They descend the walkway to six waiting stretch limousines. Ben cannot believe his eyes! His mother's among the group! "That's my mom!" he shouts pointing to her image on the monitor as tears stream slowly from the corners of his eyes. She looks amazing, as do the others! Everyone wears a pearly smile! It's amazing! It's incredible! Everyone's healthy and many years have fallen away from them! *"How can this be?" he ponders along with everyone else!*

Many had suffered from a number of debilitating illnesses, some incurable and fatal. Still others had been physically handicapped! "I believe I've witnessed an actual miracle!" Ben comments "Ruizzo? How did you know that something was happening here?" Eaton probes. "Because my 'mom' called me! Wished me a happy birthday! Told me how much she and dad loved me and how proud they're of me! She also told me that Monica's a keeper and to do the right thing! Mind you, my 'mom' has suffered with Alzheimer's and been paralyzed, waist down from a stroke for eleven years!" George Hanson's the lead agent in charge and speechless at his words for a long moment! "We've put out an APB on the vehicles. But it's as if they've simply vanished! The vehicles do not appear on any traffic cams. The only fact we know is that sixty-five are unharmed and better off now than they were hours ago!" Ben turns away from George and Eaton and starts walking to his car. Eaton hollers, "Where're you going?" "Man, I'm going home and toast my 'mom' with a scotch on the rocks! I'm happy to have seen her and to see how happy and healthy she is! This has been the best birthday ever! She told me to let her go! Now, I understand her message! You guys can spin your wheels looking for them, but you're never going to find them! She wants me to be as happy as they are! So I'm going to buy 'the ring'! Then I'm going to find Monica wherever she is, propose to her and pray that she says 'yes'!" Eaton gives an understanding nod and thumbs up gesture, "Good-luck man! Congratulations! It's about time!" As he's traveling along the driveway away from the facility he notices vehicles traveling toward it at more than a moderate speed! They're not law enforcement or media! *They're family members that've also received early morning calls of love, thanks, best wishes and farewell!*

Meanwhile, back at the 'White Dove', Agent George and Ms. Webster instruct all employees that they're under 'gag order'. However, the lid cannot be kept on this! It's occurring at nursing facilities across the Americas and several countries.

Ben had requested a copy of the video from Allison Webster before leaving. She'd easily consented hoping he'll be one less filing a lawsuit. But a lawsuit was the last thing on his mind! He wants the video to share the memory of his mother with Monica. And maybe future children!

CHAPTER TWENTY-FIVE

OFFICIAL PRESS UPDATE

JUNE 23RD
9:49 a.m. EST
Washington, D. C.
Press Room

*E*arly morning reports stated that C.O.T.A. and the Elephant congressional and senate members have been stricken with the 'POX', quarantined and that conference rooms and assembly chambers are being decontaminated and sterilized. How easily the 'Elephants' continue to lie! Oddly, the Mules are un-effected!

There's much commotion as sound men of various networks hurriedly, but carefully position their equipment in the over-packed room. The loud hum of journalists and reporters conversations in various languages fills the air. All await the N.I.A. (National Intelligence Agency) director, Patrick McCleery to take the podium. He's the one who's summoned them. Already he's received snippets of information regarding an unusually high number of unexplained deaths occurring in Africa! Communications go black on the continent before he's the opportunity to contact any embassy for more confirming information! *'They're weeding the garden!' he thinks to himself.* It's his task to put the lid on what's actually occurring as clandestine intelligence agents scramble to find answers.

10:15 a.m. The room grows 'piss cotton' quiet as he steps to the podium! *He exhales deeply.* "This morning at 5:20 a.m. congressional and senate members were rushed to John Hoskins Medical Center suffering high fevers, vomiting and body blisters. It's been determined that it's not 'chicken pox', but a more complex, debilitating virus! The CDC's taken samples to analyze. Now regarding the elderly restorations. We're extremely joyful for the seniors and their families! They've been through so much! At this time there're no answers! *He looks directly into the cameras.* We beg all who've gathered and are congregating or camped out at the various facilities and private homes to please leave these areas. Return to your own homes immediately! You're creating unnecessary health and traffic hazards and contributing to the existing chaotic atmosphere that threatens to impede routine operations. As to the burn victims, we've no answers! The numbers are striking and disturbing! Investigative teams have been dispatched. This will be the last conference at this location until the sterilization of the 'People's House' has been completed." Hands of the press dart into the air! Each hoping to get the coveted point of his finger! *Bob Stauffer of the syndicated Dailey News receives the first point!*

Bob Stauffer- "Good-morning sir! Has the type of drug administered to the elderly been identified? Could this have been an act of terrorism or an illegal drug trial?"

McCleery- "No. At the moment it hasn't been identified. But we're inspecting all pharmaceutical research laboratories, manufacturing facilities and reviewing their project data. To answer your second question, we're investigating those possibilities."

Walter Mifkinn of the Morning Express abruptly blurts, "Director! Why wasn't everyone cured? What was the determining factor?"

If looks could indeed kill Mifkinn would've dropped dead from McCleery's scornful glare!

McCleery- "It's early! The investigations are just underway!" he states raising his voice a tad! *Jim O'Brien of the Herald gets the second point.*

Jim O'Brien- "Good-morning, director! Is COTA aware of the events? And there's growing speculation that the miracles have an air of Divinity about them!"

McCleery- "Of course, he knows! Just like the rest of the world! He doesn't live in a shell nor is he buried in a hole!" 'You sure about that?' someone heckles. 'Could've fooled me!' adds another. *The room fills with laughter! If this is an angelic event it's great news! It means I'll be retiring early?" Again there's laughter! Carron Finnegan of the East Coast Guardian receives the third and final point.*

Carron Finnegan- "Good-morning, director! Sir, this magnanimous act of compassion and generosity executed with such surgical precision's clearly a demonstration of immense intelligence! Might this be an extra-terrestrial gift? *She's distracted by the vibration of her phone and looks down. The Director's phone also begins vibrating. He retrieves it from his pocket and reads its screen. By this time the phones of the others in the room are vibrating too!* Re-focusing her attention she probes, "Director? What about the sex re-assignments?" *She suspects a cover-up!*

McCleery's disposition's been one of faux calm. But both inquiries are highly charged and shake him to the core! He'd hoped to get off the podium without mentioning the reassignments or having to address them! He's more nervous now and his eyes once fixed straight ahead now wander about the room! No one takes notice except her and Jim. It's in this moment they realize she'd hit a nerve! He attempts to make light of her inquiry.

McCleery- "Ms. Finnegan! I'd appreciate it greatly if you and O'Brien stopped sharing Irish coffee first thing in the morning! Seems the whis-key part makes the two of you a little looney!" *There're a few chuckles for a second which grows to silence as the level of suspicion rises at his obvious attempt at deflection! Now it's certain something's being hidden! But what? McCleery* quickly vacates the podium and exits the room.

Later in the day, there's another development! In North Americas and around the world regardless of ethnicity, age or location females, whose gestation period began after April 30th are experiencing 'miscarriages' (involuntary abortions)! Strangely what expels or is extracted is not a fetus, but a mass of flesh and blood the size of a small plum! After the last 'live' birth at midnight, December 30th, there'll be no more for a generation.

CHAPTER TWENTY-SIX
locus angeli

JUNE 23RD
conference room
11:30 a.m.

They've viewed reports from around the world and McCleery's press briefing. The atmosphere in the room's charged with uncommon energy! The monitors are de-activated at 11:40 a.m. and the room's silent. Doe looks about group. "Well! We're off to an excellent start! Present data indicates success exceeding our projections! For the moment let's take a break! I need to speak with my 'Commanders' (*the feminine*)!" The communication dock suddenly activates and the images of Tamesh and Mobahi appear and they're laughing! "What's so funny?" Nate inquires. Laughingly she answers, "Oh, don't mind Bahi! We've been laughing at the 'sagging' victims ever since the first report! Every element of your strategy's brilliant! But the organ re-assignment! That's golden!" "Well! We (the feminine) must confess. Those antics were the brain-twins of the males!" Doe informs. Mobahi smiles broadly, "Ko, Grant, Hakeem, Michael and Nate you've made us stand tall before the D.O.O., the ORS and the universe! You've done our bonah honor! Your revenge for their cruel and un-warranted treatment of the feminine is most fitting! Bravo!" The guys offer gratitude for his praise! "ALL wanted you to know your work's outstanding and ALL are honored! Now carry-on!" bid Tamesh and Mobahi still laughing as their images fade!

Smiling Ivory looks about to each of them, "Wow! That was great!" *Referring to the high praise they've just received! Lauren rises from her seat.* "Where're you going?" Ivory questions. Lauren gives her the *look*, "I'm going to the 'Cloud'. You heard the Commander! She needs to speak with us! Plus, I need to exhale, I'm hungry and I really need a drink! A 'Lotus' to be specific!" "Hmm! That sounds good! Want some company?" "Why, of course!" *Doe overhears and interjects.* "Want me to mix and pour?" They look to each other and smile approval. Claire and Jae trail in behind.

As they enter the monitors along its walls display more news of the phenomenon and clips of the 'maniac' spewing yet more ludicrous statements and lies that unnerves the world! Doe peers at them with a distinct element of disgust that Jae detects. Swiftly she de-activates them. *The others take notice!* Doe moves behind the bar, mixes and serves each.

Ivory's on her third sip, "Hey? Did any of you check out the 'Handmaid' movie? The ideology suggested by and in its content was just crazy! Completely off the chart! To attempt to portray the feminine as objects was and is, just wrong! And the 'Incel' thing's just another bridge too far! Whichever moppet it may be that thinks this is the solution needs to clear the list first." They look to her puzzled. "What list?" "Its got about fifteen items on it, first, Got a job? 2. You got monster breath 3. Brush your teeth 4. Your speech's s-o urban! 5. Don't know how to use proper utensils for eating out 6. Morally deficient 7. I.Q almost as low as the ogre and that's just the few I remember off the top!" *The bar erupts with laughter!* As she's pouring the last glass of the third round full she looks about them, "Anyone having any doubts? *The room's quiet.* There's no reason for concern! Tauri minds are opening! There won't be a 'blue wave' in November. It'll be a Tauri tsunami! Those of decency, character and self-respect have had enough! Time to restore our national and international dignity! After the next election the 'People's House' will be blue again with feminine leadership! Time to elect respectable, compassionate, dignified candidates able to restore our respect and re-build trust with our allies and the world. For the first time there'll be Tauri feminine as C.O.T.A. and Vice C.O.T.A. The Tauri populous of the North Americas are poised to stand strong and true in support of the native Indians and adopting their values for *Earth*." "Well, what about the others, the 'children'?" Angela probes. Doe's confused by her question, "Of which children do you speak?" "You know the 'LGBTQ' kids!" Doe smiles! "Oh! They're Tauri without question! They truly reflect Almadians! They've nothing to worry! I want to remind of the rescue of the outcasts coming soon. We've 'Kirkbride' properties and others, Athens State hospital, Ancorra Psychiatric, Buffalo State, Cherokee State, Danvers, Mass., Ferguson, Minn., Poughkeepsie, N.Y., Washington, D.C., Traverse City, Mich., Weston, W. Va., Augusta, Ma., Columbia, S.C., Tuscaloosa, Ala., Hopkinsville, Ky., and Bolivar, Tn., you may recognize some of the names. They're hospitals from a time gone by, but perfectly suited for our purposes regarding housing in consideration of the numbers we must accommodate. I need reports from your units by tomorrow at this time. Um…since Hakeem and Ko are leaving tomorrow night, I'd like to suggest that everyone take leisure today! Do your own thing! In the morning we'll meet in 'Parrot Bay' for breakfast say 10:30 or so?" Everyone nods agreement.

CHAPTER TWENTY-SEVEN
anomaly i

Fifteen miles east outside the city proper of Ryaahdi, is the El Ahabib Observatory. A new planetarium. It houses the most advance examples of scientific ingenuity and technology in telescopes. Zeiss-902 - the diameter of its main mirror's 160 cm and the AZT-15. Its main mirror's 140 cm. Serenaded by the electronic melody of the machines seated in captain recliners, surrounded by monolithic monitors that lend the illusion they're floating amidst the stars are Drs. Isaiah Buhari and Amalee Dashar. They share a deep passion to discover worlds beyond our own. Their combined genius is a complimenting factor lending high probability toward their success. They've been a team for five years! Amalee backs his chair away from the console a tad, stretches and checks his watch. "Hmmp! Eye, time's really slipped by!" (Eye was the nickname he'd given Isaiah) Eye glances at the time, 11:59:34, shakes his head in mock defeat and comments, "Just another routine shift! Oh well! Maybe tomorrow! The guys (referring to their reliefs, Drs. Martin Sakara and Fahreed Basheer) will be here soon."

Their attention's drawn to a sudden unusual buzzing from the area of the printers. They vacate their seats, move towards it and see pages rapidly expelling onto already formed mounds that're growing! Unfamiliar symbols and odd characters whizz across the paper, line by line, at laser speed! The indicator lights of the telescopes control panels display variations of patterns and sequences! Each moves to a printer and gathers a portion of the accumulated mound. They carry them over to the work table and begin to pour over the text with their backs to the monitors. A few minutes pass before they look up from the printed data to each other. "I can't believe it's happening!" Amalee remarks giddy. Eye smiles back, "Oh! Believe it my friend! They've sent a message! And we have it!" At that moment the room lights up as day! They look to each other in disbelief! As they turn they can't believe the spectacle before their eyes! They're in awe!

They return to their seats. It's a spectacular sight! Every star has a blinding white, bluish tinged halo of intricate design, each distinctly different from the other like snowflakes! This was real! No evidence of moisture or dust interfering with the transmission or on the targeted area Contact from another life form has not only occurred! But provided a display for the world to see!

At 00:18:59 (the 24th) the printers go silent and the halos disappear from the night skies over Egypt, Africa, but manifest in other skies according to time zones. Eye and Amalee just sit stunned in contemplation for a while! The phone hasn't rung and there've been no computer generated messages of alert or priority. The visual anomaly's public! But the transmissions appear to have been received only by them! Their concern quickly shifts to the safety of their loved ones! Their secondary concern's whether or not to share the existence of the printed data with their 'reliefs' or governmental agencies. With trust at an all-time low they decide to collect all printed data, drives and opt to conceal them. They didn't like withholding information, but this was too important to get wrong! They'd wait! See what the day would bring. However, as a precaution Eye suggests that they move their families to safety immediately! He picks up the phone and dials a number. It rings and a voice answers, "Yeah?" "It's me! Buhari! I need to move my family and that of my colleague to safety ASAP!" After nodding several times he returns the phone to its cradle and looks to Amalee. "We'll be moved to safety within the hour. We're to tell them there's a security threat and that the move's just a precautionary procedure." "Thank-you, Eye!" "Thank me for what? We're a team!" Amalee tries to conjure a smile. They hear the heavy slam of the door and the footfalls of their reliefs as they climb the iron steps.

June 24th 00:18 a.m. GMT

Meanwhile at the 'Greenwood'

The event's captured by its surveillance systems. The senior officer on duty alerts Tamesh and Mobahi of the activity and transmits the data to them. After reviewing the footage of the anomaly they look to one another. Mobahi's voice carries a tone of uncanny peace, "Well, Tamesh! *He exhales deeply.* The prophecy's unfolding on our watch!" "Yes it is." "Should we alert the *seedlings*?" "Yes! We will, but I *sense* we should wait! This event feels like a signal, a preview of something more significant to come! It feels like there's a '*tell*'! Let's wait! Mobahi this is only the *show*! But *we* should contact-" she's interrupted by the sound of an incoming 'vc' alert. It's Jonas. And he's smiling as his image appears! "How're things?" His smile disappears as he notes their solemn demeanor. They glance to each other then look to him. She exhales and her tone's measured, "We were just about to contact you! Jonas, the Blue Star Kachina's arrived! He's stunned to silence and his eyes roam about respectively. "What's it look like? Is it beautiful? Can you show me the visual?" he begs fighting to suppress his excitement! Mobahi smiles, "It's spectacular! It's wondrous! But you must wait! Witness it for yourself at midnight! I know you've got a bit of a wait! A little over six hours if I'm correct! But I promise you'll understand the insistence of my actions!" "Wow! Alright! Is there anything we should be doing?" "No! We must wait! However, it might behoove us to ratchet up production of the 'Auton'! We must protect them!" Tamesh suggests. "I agree! No worries! We'll prepare! I'll check back later. Be well!"

CHAPTER TWENTY-EIGHT
anomaly ii

Phase Two
JUNE 24TH
2:37 a.m. (time zone specific)

All weapons and ammunition manufacturing plants, stores of distribution, warehouses, storage spaces and casinos around the world are given a ten minute warning to vacate. At the eleventh minute all targets are alit by blinding illuminations! There're no sounds of explosion. It lasts less than three minutes! When the light wanes all of the targets are gone! Parking lots and vehicles gone as well as people if they hadn't heeded the warning! All that remains are grassy, tree filled spaces!

Even privately owned firearms have been neutralized! There's not a firearm on *Earth* that will fire! *No agency on Earth detected the transmitted wave responsible for melting the firing pins of weapons in pick-up trucks, private clubs and residences!*

CHAPTER TWENTY-NINE
the cell

JUNE 25TH
Hastings, Nebraska
11:30 a.m. CMT

Big Sky country was no exaggeration in description when it came to this place! Its ninety degrees, the sky's sapphire blue with scattered white clouds and a beaming sun! The snow-capped mountain peaks in the distance add to the majesty of the sight as George Jobakowski and Joe Flannery ride into the field. George's the day shift foreman for the K-13 sector of the ZXL pipeline and Joe's the inspecting engineer. Both are employed by the Apollo Fuel Company. They travel as far as they can along the dirt road before it ends and they're forced to park and proceed on foot along a well-worn path. It leads to the wrought iron platform where the system controls are located. "Whew!" George exclaims wiping perspiration from his brow with a towel. He grimaces with disgust as they climb the steps onto the landing. "Joe! What is that? The shits awful! Man! It's worse than sewage!" Both place their hands over their nose and mouth as they proceed attempting to avoid inhaling the stench. They're stunned by what they see! Instead of the routine white and green pulsating indicator lights they're standing emergency red! Joe walks over to the east corner, looks down the line and sees nothing. But he does hear an unfamiliar sound and hollers to George, "Hey! Come over here and listen!" George moves to him and nods after listening for a moment, "Yeah! I do hear something. But what is it? Come on! Let's walk the line." They grab binoculars out of a drawer of the console, descend and begin walking along the line. Fifteen minutes into their inspection they're paralyzed at the terrifying sight before them

170

and source of the stench! Black crude's flowing from a rupture the length of two city buses and the breath of semi cab! Thru the binoculars they see a black carpet stretching at least half a mile before them! "Christ!" Joe swears loudly. "They refused to listen!" yells George as he hangs his head in his hand. "Mary Mother of God! What have we done?"

Simultaneously, miles away on the Japanese island of Kyushu it's 1:30 a.m. GMT.

Forty miles outside the city of Fukuoka, in the province of Yo Hon, gentle winds blow thru the most magnificent exotic garden. In the midst of this paradise is the shinden-zukuri of Mitsuaki and Mai Oshiro. The parents of eight year old 'Ai'.

Still asleep she rises from her bed, walks to the middle of the room, sits down and assumes the Lotus position! Tears cascade down her soft, plump cheeks and her body begins to rise. She ascends four feet from the floor before halting and floating cloud-like! Yarn-like strands of energy exudes from her chest and extend three feet in front of the young one. They begin to intertwine and rotate counter-clock wise creating a beach ball size mass. It tappers off, her tears cease and the mass floats thru the *now open* window, descends to the ground and is absorbed by *Earth*. Ai's infusing *Earth*! She's a star-child! She hears *her* cries of distress and feels *her* pain more acutely than the others!

Mai begins to toss and turn in her sleep, hearing music that's not consistent with her dream. She awakes and glances at the time, 1:51 a.m. She sits up. That's when she realizes the melody's coming from inside the shinden-zukuri! She eases off of the bed, careful not to awaken Mitsuaki. Tiptoes over to the chair, grabs and hurriedly wrestles into her kimono then eases over to the door and gently slides it open. She walks the house searching for the source. As she nears Ai's room she notices a glow emanating thru the spaces about and under her door! She hears no sounds of distress, only the melody that's becoming more soothing! Delicately she slides Ai's door open. Reflexively her hand covers her mouth to smother

her shrieks of shock and amazement! Ai's suspended in the air, resting on what resembles a cloud! She turns and hurries back to wake Mitsuaki. "Aki! Get up!" *He stirs.* "Aki! Get up, it's Ai!" she begs frantically. His eyes open, "What's wrong?" he mumbles. Then he hears the melody and looks to her, "Is that Ai?" *She nods.* Aki rushes out of the room. In the moments it'd taken her to awaken him an invisible barrier had formed at her door! Feeling helpless he grabs Mai's hand, "What do we do?" "There's nothing we need to do! She's not harmed nor in distress. All we can do's wait!" The phone in the hall begins to ring. She moves to it. Her voice is noticeably guarded as she answers, "Konnichiha." "Konnichiha, Mai! What's happening with Ai? Is she alright? *It's Kaye Richardson of Los Angeles, California in North Americas. They share a unique relationship because of their children. She's the mother of Kahlon, another star-child.* Mai? Are you alright?" "Kaye? Where're you? How's Kahlon?" "We're at the Center. *The Center's a privately owned genetic research facility.* Everything was routine until 10:30 a.m. Then Kahlon suddenly stopped interacting, started chanting and a most beautiful melody filled the space about him! He's sitting on some type of cloud at the moment and the melody continues!" "It's the same with Ai!" "Mai! Calls are pouring in from the other parents too! It's obvious the kids are sharing and synchronized with each other! But what does it mean? Everyone here's amazed! The doctors and technicians are scrambling, gathering and analyzing data in an effort to understand what's happening! I don't fear for the children! I'm terrified by what they apparently know and will tell us!" "Kaye, nothing of this magnitude's ever occurred! Strangely, I feel very calm…at peace!" "Me too! Mai! Now go! Attend to your family and try to record what you can. How's Aki taking this?" "He's shaken a bit! But he'll be fine. Thanks for your concern! Talk with you later." Kaye takes a few calming breaths as she looks off and ponders, '*This is a sign. But of what?*'

Presently, there're one hundred confirmed star children, also referred to as indigo or crystal, spanning five continents and twenty nations. They're mildly affected by some events, but completely reactionary to those that directly impact *her...Earth!* Their small hearts are heavy with grief for *her,* but they'll sustain *her* until 'The ONE' comes to her aid.

10:30 a.m. PST

Military air stations and bases of the North Americas and around the world haven't recorded any anomalies since an uncharted chunk of a meteor fell into the Pacific Ocean six months ago. At 10:30 a.m. (PST) the small cone-shaped emergency lights that hang from the ceilings in various installations awaken from dormancy and begin to twirl vigorously and glow bright red! Sirens scream eminent danger! The seismic detection equipment of global geological facilities register unprecedented activity! Yet, the *Earth* hasn't convulsed nor has there been loss of life! The radar screens in the North Americas and around the world display radiating patterns and indicate a point of origin- Californias, county of San Bernardino, City of Big Bear Lake.

Breaking news interrupts all broadcasts! BMBC correspondent Tammi Hall's on the scene reporting from Big Bear Lake, "You're seeing the ambulance carrying a body of an unidentified male being escorted by the California State Highway Patrol at is front and rear. The north-bound direction of traffic has been shut down on the highway leading out of Big Bear Lake to the expressway as well as I-40. The rumor mill speculates its 'The ONE' who's being rushed to the nearest medical facility. He's been leasing an extravagant estate in the area while awaiting completion of Wonderland's construction."

'The One's a gifted composer, choreographer, singer, songwriter and the world's greatest entertainer of the 20th century! He's attempted to champion the minds of reasonable humanoids! Many who were directly responsible for the perpetration of atrocities against nature, against *her!* But they refused to heed his warnings! 'The ONE' possessed the ability to transfuse energy to *her.* He'd been spiritually attached to *her* and granted the privilege to commune directly with *her* from his birth!

From the moment his body's loaded into the ambulance there're no births or deaths! For two hours while attempts are being made to save his life the world's at total peace!

Despite all efforts he passes onto the next plane causing a violent rip between their spirits! *Her* pain's so intense it causes the activation of the 'fail-safe' which expels the 'IDWD' (*invisible distress wave device*)! It's a galactic flare…a type of S.O.S!

The '*fail-safe* device was constructed of *Phakilran* materials. Its dimensions were 20x36. Similar in dimensions to a four drawer file cabinet, but a few inches wider. It housed a projectile that resembles a cucumber with spikes. It'd been buried, in a ship, deep within *Earth* during *her* infancy before fragmentation in the place now known as Texas in North Americas, four hundred miles away from El Paso in an area known as the 'zona del silencio', Zone of Silence. Its programmed destination's *Phakilra*. However, the powerful, quasonic signal it emits will be detected by others, thru out the galaxies and forwarded to *Phakilra* long before the 'IDWD' itself arrives there. Upon notice of the signal immediate preparations begin for launch to *her* rescue! They're coming in great haste for *their beloved*! They're coming for *Earth*!

1:05 p.m. EST

Locus Angeli, Caicos, Turks Islands

Outside the 'Cloud' puffy white clouds fill the azure sky and a gentle breeze blows. Inside they lounge about. In the blink of an eye the room becomes colder than a morgue! They begin to shiver! An icy wind fills the room and their exhalations stream from their nostrils like steam! They look to each other wide-eyed as they shiver uncontrollably and teeth chatter! Suddenly the wind ceases, the temperature in the room rises and a warm sensation washes over them starting at the soles of their feet traveling upward to the top of their heads! After a few moments it wanes. The 'cd' behind the bar begins to ring. Mano answers. After listening intently he nods, disengages and announces, "They await you in the 'Consilium'. They're still shaken from what's just occurred as they rise and exit the room.

Their postures are rigid and their faces bear despondent expressions as the group enters. "Good-morning, Tamesh, Mobahi!" "It's not a good-morning. I needed you together because I only have the strength to say this once." *Her tone's grievous and their oculi are sad!* "What's wrong?" Doe challenges. Tamesh realizes they're unaware of the news or what's occurred by their inquiry! "Obviously, you've not seen the breaking news! *As a rule of their nature they don't watch earthly broadcasts and when they do its ecological programming such as 'Earth from above' or 'What on Earth'! To them it's depressing and concerning the negatives occurring rather than the good!* The worst has occurred! They've succeeded in fatally wounding *her*! *She's* dying!" *They're speechless! That explains what they'd just experienced. It'd been Her!*

"Well! Can 'The One' support *her* while *she* regenerates?" Ivory probes. "That was the hope! But 'The One's' been fatally assaulted too!" "Tah? Do the young ones know?" With saddened spirit and watery eyes Tamesh looks to her, "They were first! However, despite their grief they're aiding *her*! We only hope they can endure and *she* holds on! She's cherished by the D.O.O., the Almadians, the entire Mahos galaxy and the universe! Someone's coming to *her* rescue! The mission's been drastically altered. It's shifted to not only protecting the Tauri, but to prepare them for assimilation. They're not responsible for their plight! Their generations have been victims! We must prepare with diligence and haste, due to the instability of *her* condition! *She'll* continue to fight as *she's* taught all of *her daughters* to do! Special focus must now be placed on the orientation of the feminine regarding their status and handling their 'powers' soon to manifest. It's of great need and advantage to begin nurturing their minds to ensure a smooth transition as the effect of the conversion causes the awakening of their 'KSCs'. For that reason Phase III is to be implemented immediately! You're tasked with the responsibility of constantly reminding the Tauri of the North Americas and the world how closely intertwined they're despite the logistical distances between them. All are suffering various circumstances of difficult challenges and struggles from a greater or lesser degree! The world's beyond frustration with the populous of the North Americas! They look to them for leadership and strength! Now's the time for…how do you say? Uh…step to the hole?" *The room erupts into chuckles!* Tah's expression's one of confusion! Ivory quickly whispers to her, "Highness! Um… It's step up to the plate." "Oh!" she chuckles and nods before continuing. "Due to the circumstances attached to its existence, 'North Americas' has become the beacon of hope and the hammer of peace for the world. Unfortunately, all of its populous bears and shares the weight of guilt in one way or another allowing for the grotesque BT idiot to be elected by another group of misguided BTs! Who've been coerced by the Russians to cast their 'electorial' votes for him, because he couldn't win the popular vote! *(No one's investigated these persons nor checked their finances before and after the election to know if they'd been coerced!)* His disdain for *Earth's* very evident in his decisions, orders and in keeping with the Bahleide philosophy… his bonah!" Mobahi senses her emotional weariness, "My Queen! Allow me to finish." She nods permissive.

He continues, "Tauri must also be fully informed as to the identity of the Russian that has so much power and control over the 'mad ogre' and directs so much havoc across the globe. They must understand he's the epitome of an evil genius! He's not a BT! He's not even humanoid! He's a Bahleide! The unrest that's occurring around the world now is at his direct order and is but a small part of a much larger plan he devised years ago before attaining the position of absolute power. For the past sixteen years he's been orchestrating it bit by bit, like weaving a fine tapestry. North Americas gave him the best gift ever with the election of the 'mad ogre'! He couldn't have planned it any better or wanted for more! Now he's the perfect idiot to do his bidding as C.O.T.A. and he salivates with the thought like a starved animal! He feels he's at the precipice of world domination! Europeans well understand what he and political females/males like him are and what they bring! They've not only had it at their front door, but in the backyard! Those in the Americas haven't experienced war in their land since the Civil War! However, they inch closer to its experience unless they wake-up and react! None can afford to be complacent! They must be made to understand that! The only obstacle in his way now are the Tauri of the Americas and the world! Their numbers are great and growing stronger! They must stand! All power's in their collective hands! They must save *Earth* in order to have a future!

North America's's been hit by an environmental, political and social tsunami...the obese ogre! He's granted permission to BT oil barons that'll cause *her* more damage! He's caused destruction equal to a monster wave in people's lives at home and abroad! Yet, he stands numb to the pain and misery he's caused and is causing! He's ignorant to the life of everyday people who must toil for their existence! He spins the lie that the elephants are the party of healthcare! All the while making every effort to dismantle the basic security the people have! He's no plan! The party's no plan! His ideal offering would be a first aid kit with a few bandages, an Ace bandage, a roll of sterile gauze, a couple of packets of Alcodine and maybe an aspirin! The Alcodine would be the most valuable part of the kit! After all of the havoc the 'mad ogre' has visited upon the people of this land and terrible policies, or lack of, in other lands, a second term's no longer thinkable! Tauri have had enough! United they will stand and elect 'mule' senators, C.O.T.As and maintain the mule congress. Then and only then can healing begin. There'll be no new life (births) on *Earth* until the last child born grows into full maturity and independence. Within this time span two billion people will pass on. It'll be of great relief to *Earth* to have the burden of so many lifted from *her*! You must help them understand that their very existence is at stake and they must unite to save *Earth* for their survival! It's the only path to healing! All must be for peace! From hence forth *Earth* must be first priority!

The Bilderberg Group, Free Masons, Illuminati and Opus Dei are 'secret societies' controlled and headed by actual Bahleide. All of the despots have seats at these tables. The memberships of these groups are both

BTs and low level Bahleide. Together they gather once a year at Bohemian Grove. The Bahleide and the BTs know there's only ONE and that's the D.O.O! For their deceit they've earned the punishment of extinction!" "Extinction?" Hakeem questions. Mobahi gives a positive nod and exhales, "Yes, Hakeem! You've not witnessed their countenance nor enormity of their being! But when you do! You'll understand! They're cannibals and they do, literally, eat their own! They'll descend upon the Tauri like bull-dog ants and consume all in their way. They'll put some on display zoo-like! They'll store some for future feed, enslave others and may even dig up the recent dead! They're maggots! They've been spicing up humanoids for generations hoping for the chance to feed! What'd you think all the 'legal' prescription drug pushing was and is about?" she challenges low spirited. Who do you think runs big 'pharma'? Drugs are nothing more than spices to the humanoid body for them! They create illnesses then supposedly create and offer miracle drugs to combat their affects! Drugs whose side-effects are worse than their illness! They provide technology detrimental to a society ill prepared for it! For the past two hundred years people around the globe have gone and continue to go about their daily life routine with little regard for nature and no true focus on *her*! Many are too consumed with fame, glamour, glitter, devices, gadgets, money and other intangible things while others struggle day to day just to live! The accessories of life mean nothing if you can't breathe the air, drink the water, there's no grain to consume, nothing will grow and livestock's diseased! The Tauri have lost their discipline! They must reclaim it and lift their heads from the hole in the sand! It hasn't always been like this! Well, we'll leave you to your work!" *Their images fade.*

They look about the room to each other in silence. Their mission's been drastically altered! Their focus's not only to protect the Tauri, but to prepare them. Rescue's coming for *Earth*! Not for them! It's the time of 'FULFILLMENT'!

EARTH WAS NOT CREATED FOR HUMANOIDS
THEY WERE CREATED FOR HER

GLOSSARY OF TERMS

A.I.A. - Americas Intelligence Agency

Alcodine- a 22nd century external topical antibiotic treatment with internal applications, invented in New Jersey by a gifted bio-chemist.

Auton- pronounced (all-tun) – genetically engineered enzyme that dissolves fatty build up, activates and simulates the gray matter

Bahleide- pronounced (buh-lee-dae')

Bahwei- pronounced (bah` way) - a fluxuating field of time

Bonah- pronounced (boo-nah) –of same species, family

Clusterhub-mobile units of operations

Delik- pronounced (dell-eek) – measure of time approximately equivalent to an Earth year.

ERC- environmental respiratory congestion

ERA- environmental respiratory arrest

F.I.B. - Federal Intelligence Bureau

fugly- slang for f**king ugly

GEBI-genetically engineered bionic insects. Their structural frames are infused with a liquid that's titanium-type properties. They've two electronic eyes three times smaller than a pin head. Nano transponders provide tracking and vision control. Their stingers are thinner than a single strand of hair. Their abdominal sections carry a strange deadly venom.

Heloose- pronounced (heel-`oo-shi) - measurement of time equivalent to a decade on Earth

KSC- Knowledge storage centers located at the frontal section on the left-side of the cerebrum

LDTS- long distance tour syndrome

LES- life energy signature

Mahos- pronounced (may-hoss) -solar system outside of the Milky Way across the Bahwei

Maiphen- pronounced (may-finn) - a catalyst agent causing accelerated growth and cellular regeneration while dissolving the protein build-up around the KSCs

Metos- pronounced (mee-toss) - measurement of time similar to Earth hours.

Mobahi- pronounced (moe-`bah-hee)

Nahaea- pronounced (na-`hay-eh) -jelly-like colloid infused with bio-chemical enzymes that attacks, dissolves germs and dead skin cells as well as extracting oil deposits with a serotonin element. It's a complex, gratifying cleansing compound.

Nahzee- pronounced (in-`awe-zae) - A viral-type illness specific to their species brought on by sleep deprivation.

Nebis- the mid-center left region of the cerebellum

Neuba- pronounced (`knee-oo-bah)- junior officers

N.I.A. - National Intelligence Agency

ODAD- Observation, detection, atmospheric assessment devices

ORS- superior lifeforms and ambassadors of the *D.O.O.*

Phakilra- pronounced (fah-`kee-rah) – the fourth planet in the Mahos solar system

Plane of Viability (P.O.V) - a five mile sliver of space beyond the Bahwei

Pushae- pronounced (poo-shay) – vitamin supplement blended with maiphen

Quopozoest- pronounced (kway-poe-ace) - Almadian clan name

Seeding- process of gestation and birthing

Shinden-zukuri- Japanese word for home

SMV- acronym for solar powered marine vessel

Sotia- pronounced (soo-`tee-ah) –small bubble-like tennis ball size beads comprised of oxygen and credion that floats inside the P.O.V.

Tamesh- pronounced (tay-meesh)

Zauton- pronounced (zah-all'-tun) – 'star' intelligence booster

Zeatus- pronounced (zee-ay-tus) - anatomical booster

Zeltron- pronounced (zel-ron) - a spherical body. Its outer shell's comprised of a tantalum-titanium blend alloy. Its cavity's filled with a gel-like blend of uranium, plutonium and nitrogen. In the midst of this mixture's an 'I-chip'. An 'I-chip', the size of a grain of sugar, is the controlling mechanism for delivery and detonation.